ANYTHING BUT LOVE

OTHER TITLES IN THE SERIES:

Almost Like Love

Nothing Like Love

Other books by the author:

Winning the Right Brother

The Millionaire's Wish

Cross My Heart

Waiting for You

Into Your Arms

ANYTHING BUT LOVE

Abigail Strom

Montlake
Romance

Published by Montlake Romance, Seattle
www.apub.com

Amazon, the Amazon logo, and Montlake Romance are trademarks of Amazon.com, Inc., or its affiliates.

ISBN-13: 9781503936768
ISBN-10: 1503936767

Cover design by Damonza

Printed in the United States of America

For Vanessa

CHAPTER ONE

B en Taggart hated suits, social obligations, and most of the people he'd grown up with, and Jessica Bullock's wedding would be the perfect storm of all three.

The last thing he wanted to do on a summer Saturday was attend the nuptials of a woman from his Upper East Side past. He and Jessica were barely even acquaintances anymore, so why the hell was he going to her big society wedding?

Because his mother was making him. He was a grown-ass man, and he was going to put on a tie and go to this stupid shindig because he couldn't say no to his mother.

"That's adorable," Jamal Baker told him as Weisman dribbled around them both, sinking a three-pointer with ease. "I had no idea you were such a mama's boy."

Ben made the rebound and passed the ball to Jamal. "I can't help it. She's like a human ASPCA commercial. I take one look at those big sad eyes and it's all over."

Jamal dribbled toward the other basket. "Your mother has big sad eyes?"

"Like a golden retriever."

Jamal attempted what should have been an easy layup, and the ball ricocheted off the backboard.

"That was pathetic," Ben told him as Garrett made the rebound, passing the ball to Weisman.

"I know," Jamal acknowledged, panting as the two of them attempted man-to-man defense against their far more skilled opponents. "Explain to me again why we're subjecting ourselves to this humiliation?"

"Because when a former student gets drafted by the Knicks and asks if you want to join him and a teammate in a pickup game, you say yes."

"I used to admire you for getting so involved in your students' lives. Now I think it's time for you to get cynical and jaded."

Ben grinned as Garrett made a superhuman leap and dunked the ball over Jamal's head.

"And miss moments like this? No way."

Jamal called for a mercy time-out and went over to the bench where he'd left his water bottle. "You have to reconsider moving to Chicago," he said. "If you leave New York, who's going to remind me that I'm getting old and can no longer play a decent game of basketball?"

Garrett and Weisman had joined them. "I will," Garrett promised. "Right after I remind you that if you and Mr. Taggart hadn't gotten me through high school, I wouldn't be here to kick your asses."

A little while later Ben and Jamal, having graciously conceded defeat on the basketball court, were walking through Fort Tryon Park toward the 190th Street subway station. It was a beautiful June day: perfect for basketball, jogging through the park, or anything that didn't involve sitting in a church watching two people recite empty wedding vows.

"How do you know they'll be empty?" Jamal asked.

Ben used the hem of his T-shirt to wipe the lingering sweat from his forehead. "I've known Jessica for twenty years. I have no idea why she's getting married, but it's not because she's in love."

"I thought you said you haven't seen her for a while."

"So?"

"So maybe things have changed. Maybe she's fallen for someone."

"She hasn't."

"How can you be so sure?"

"Because the only person Jessica Bullock could ever really love is herself."

"Wow. Harsh."

Ben shrugged. "Like I said, I've known her a long time."

"Yeah, but aren't you the guy who's all about redemption and second chances? It's never too late to change. Isn't that what you tell the kids everyone else has given up on?"

"It's easier to reach kids who grew up with nothing than it is to convince Park Avenue royalty that there's anything wrong with the way they live."

"Correct me if I'm wrong, but aren't you a royal yourself?"

"A former royal." Ben swiped his card and pushed through the turnstile. "I'm the exception that proves the rule."

Two subway stops and a short walk later, the two men were back at their Washington Heights apartment building.

"You're coming tomorrow, right?" Jamal asked when the elevator stopped at his floor.

Ben drew a blank for a second. "Coming to—? Oh, your poetry slam. Yeah, I'll be there."

Jamal stuck his hand in front of the elevator doors to keep them from closing. "I find your lack of enthusiasm disturbing," he said in his best Darth Vader voice.

"Sorry. This wedding has me off my game."

"It's only a few hours out of your life," Jamal said, stepping out into the hallway. "How bad could it be?" he added as the elevator closed behind him.

A few minutes later, unlocking the door to his apartment, Ben asked himself the same thing.

How bad could it be?

Here was an even better question. Why was he so riled up? As Jamal had said, it would all be over in a few hours. He could cut out of the reception early and erase the memory with cheap beer in a local bar. Why was he letting this get under his skin?

He tossed his keys onto the table inside the door and went to the kitchen for a glass of water. As he passed the refrigerator, he saw the invitation his mother had stuck under a magnet the last time she'd stopped by—a gentle reminder of the event he'd promised to attend.

Mr. and Mrs. William Bullock

request the honor of your presence

at the marriage of their daughter

JESSICA ANNE

to

THOMAS HARRISON SHELBURNE

He pulled the invitation off the fridge and laid it down on the counter. As he stared at the elegant script spelling out *Jessica Anne*, two very different images came into his mind.

One was a memory of Jessica from junior high, when the two of them had still been friends. The other was a memory from high school, when they'd been enemies.

Maybe *enemies* was too strong a word. But when Jessica had come back from camp the summer before ninth grade—her parents had sent her to an exclusive fat farm for teens—she'd been like a different person.

A person who wasn't interested in his friendship anymore.

She was twenty pounds lighter and dressed in the kind of fashionable clothes she used to despise. She started wearing makeup, and she stopped talking to him.

It had taken him a few days of the new school year to realize what was happening. But the third time she walked past him in the hall without even making eye contact, he got the hint.

Jessica was making a new place for herself in high school, and he wasn't going to be part of it.

He spent the first few months of freshman year trying to find his own place. He was good at sports, but he wasn't a jock; he got good grades, but he wasn't a brain; he liked gaming and science fiction, but he wasn't a geek.

He wondered for a while if he'd always be someone who could visit different groups without ever belonging to one. But he started to make a few good friends, and after a while he realized that what they had in common wasn't what they liked but who they were: Kids who could enjoy a lot of different things but didn't want to be defined by them. Kids who would stand up to bullies and didn't care as much about being popular. Kids who knew they wanted to make a difference in the world even if they weren't sure yet how they'd do it.

With a lot of different interests and a group of new friends, Ben had enjoyed high school for the most part. His life became busy with school and activities—but that didn't mean he forgot about the friend he'd lost. The friend who'd turned her back on him.

He'd been too proud to ask her why, even though their parents' friendship had given him plenty of opportunities. At least once a month he saw her at a family function, either hers or his, but he never took advantage of the circumstances to talk to her.

He'd figured she was putting distance between herself and anything that reminded her of her "fat" past. The funny thing was, he'd found her far more beautiful when she was twenty pounds heavier. Once she was skinny and a better fit for society's definition of beauty, his feelings were a lot more complicated.

It was hard to separate her changed appearance from her apparently relentless pursuit of popularity, something that had never mattered to her before. And of course the fact that she'd turned her back on their friendship so completely was a factor, too. But as much as he'd tried to dismiss her from his mind the way she'd obviously dismissed him, he hadn't been able to.

All through high school, as much as he'd hated the person she was becoming, he couldn't make himself hate her. Somewhere under the superficial exterior she'd constructed for herself was the thirteen-year-old girl he'd had a crush on—the girl who never met a stray cat or dog she didn't try to rescue, who volunteered at the local animal shelter every weekend. He couldn't believe that the Jessica Bullock he'd known so well had just disappeared.

But the more time that passed the more it seemed she had disappeared, leaving only a beautiful shell behind. His friend had turned into an aspiring Park Avenue socialite who didn't seem to care about anything but herself.

Now she was getting married—to Tom Shelburne, of all people. Tom and Jessica had been friends since high school, but Ben had never gotten a romantic vibe from them. The only thing he knew they had in common was wealth and social prominence. Because of that, it was easier to imagine their marriage as a kind of business merger rather than a love match.

It shouldn't matter to him. But as he stared down at the invitation and remembered Jessica as she'd once been, he realized that it did matter.

Which made no damn sense at all. He hadn't even seen Jessica for a couple of years now. Watching her walk down the aisle to marry a man she probably didn't love shouldn't affect him in the slightest. So why the hell was it getting to him?

He crumpled the invitation in his hand and tossed it into the trash as he headed for the bathroom. It was time to get ready for the wedding he didn't want to go to.

Suck it up, he told himself as he turned on the shower. As Jamal had said, it was one afternoon out of his life.

A few hours and it would all be over. How bad could it be?

~

A few hours and it would all be over.

Jessica repeated the words in her head like a mantra. *A few hours and it will all be over.*

It was her wedding day, and the perfection of her physical appearance was the culmination of years of effort. Diets, exercise regimens, facials, manicures, seaweed wraps, waxing, makeup consultations . . . the list went on and on.

How many thousands of dollars had she spent on the quest for beauty over the years? If she included her wedding dress and the fat farm her parents had sent her to in junior high, she was probably close to six figures.

She was twenty-eight years old now, and it all came down to this. The ultimate photo op; the portrait that would grace her mantelpiece—and her parents' mantelpiece—for the rest of her life. She would be captured at this moment of perfection for all time.

"Jessica? Are you all right?"

It was her sister, Vicki, who ate what she wanted and didn't care what she weighed.

"What do you mean?" she asked.

Vicki came up beside her and met her eyes in the big mirror. "You were staring at yourself. Is something wrong? You look perfect."

"I know."

Vicki patted her shoulder. "That's my modest little sister. Are you ready to go? The limo's here."

Her bridesmaids chattered during the ride, but Jessica didn't join them. She stared out the window at the city passing by without seeing a thing.

That's my modest little sister.

Vicki thought she was being vain or proud by acknowledging that she looked beautiful, but she wasn't. She was only being accurate.

She *was* beautiful.

But she was beautiful like one of those elaborately decorated Ukrainian Easter eggs. As time passed, the egg inside dried out until only the shell remained. You picked one up expecting it to have weight and heft, but it was lighter than air.

Empty.

A year ago she and Tom had made a pact. They'd get married, share a home, and live separate lives under the cover of conventional normalcy.

At least Tom knew what he wanted to do with the space and freedom this false life would provide. Jessica still had no idea.

As the wedding itself approached, that was what scared her the most.

For a long time now she'd been too numb to be afraid. It had been a welcome numbness, the simple act of putting one foot in front of the other and dealing with externals. French onion soup or walnut goat cheese salad? Swing band or rock and roll? Pale pink or dark pink for the ribbons on the centerpieces?

8

There had been a certain satisfaction in those details. They had given her something to focus on—a distraction from the emptiness inside her. Her perfectionism found an outlet in the obsessive world of wedding planning, and for a year, that had been her whole world . . . along with renovating and decorating the apartment she and Tom would live in.

Now all that work was done. The apartment was finished; the wedding ceremony was imminent. Tomorrow morning she and Tom would head to Bermuda for their honeymoon, which she was actually looking forward to.

But after the honeymoon?

She had no idea.

For now, though, numbness was still her friend. Or at least, it was until they arrived at the church and the minister greeted her with a smile, showing her and the bridal party to the private room where they would wait for their cue.

She wasn't just lying to her family and friends. She was lying to God.

Religion had never played a big role in her life, but something about that phrase—lying to God—pierced her heart somehow.

Her mother was bustling around, fussing with bouquets and the bridesmaids' hair. Every so often she said to Jessica, "Just keep breathing, sweetheart. You're doing great."

Heather, the only one of her bridesmaids who was married, squeezed Jessica's hand. "I was a nervous wreck before my wedding. I remember shaking like a leaf and being terrified I'd trip or drop my bouquet, but of course it wasn't really about that. It's the getting married part that freaks a person out. Even when you're marrying the man of your dreams, it's still pretty scary."

Jessica gave Heather the same mechanical smile she'd given her mother. It was obvious that any tension in her demeanor was being put down to nerves.

But then Simone Oliver put a hand on her shoulder.

Simone had been one of her college roommates. She wasn't the kind of person Jessica had associated with in high school, but they'd become friends freshman year—and in spite of many surface differences, they'd stayed friends ever since.

"Hey, Jess—can I talk to you for a sec?"

"Now?"

"It won't take long."

"Well . . . all right."

Simone led her far enough away from the others that they wouldn't be overheard.

"You probably already know this, but Tom's a great guy. He's smart and sweet and funny, and I think it's wonderful that you're going to marry him." She gripped Jessica's arm. "But hypothetically speaking . . . if there's anything making you unhappy, any reason you don't want to get married . . . well, then, we can get the hell out of here. We can hit the ATM and take a cab to Florida. We can hop a freight train and ride the rails to California. Whatever you need."

Jessica didn't say anything for a moment or two. When she did speak, her voice shook a little. "Wouldn't that be a nice story for page six. I can see the headline now: 'Park Avenue Princess Turns Runaway Bride.' "

"So what if they say that? Who gives a damn? This is your life, Jessica. That's all that matters."

Jessica stared at her. Simone had figured out, somehow, that something was wrong—and she was offering a way out. For one crazy minute, she actually thought about saying yes.

But even if she were willing to do that to her parents, she couldn't do it to Tom.

She shook her head slowly. "I can't. I can't. I . . ." She shook her head again. "Tom and I have been friends forever. I do love him, even if it's not . . ." She stopped. "I love him," she said again. "And I feel safe with him. I made a promise, and I—"

The door to the waiting room opened and one of the ushers stuck his head in. "They're ready for you, ladies."

There was last-minute primping and excited whispers as the bridal party headed for the door. Simone started to join them, but Jessica grabbed her hand first.

"I want you to know I won't forget this. I mean . . . that was a really nice offer."

"I offered to help you ditch your own wedding," Simone reminded her.

Jessica smiled crookedly. "I know. I just . . . thank you. You're a good friend."

Simone gave her a careful hug, avoiding her hair, makeup, and dress. "You're a good friend, too. And Tom's a great guy."

Jessica took a deep breath. "He is, isn't he? And I do love him."

"All right, then. Let's get you married."

CHAPTER TWO

B en couldn't sit still. He was restless and nothing seemed to help.

His mother was sitting next to him in the crowded pew. "What's wrong with you?" she hissed from behind her wedding program.

"Nothing."

Tom Shelburne stepped up to the altar along with the minister, best man, and a troop of groomsmen. The organist began the processional. The wedding guests dutifully turned their heads, and here came a flock of bridesmaids.

Ben's mind, as restless as his body, started playing with collective nouns. A parliament of owls, an ostentation of peacocks, an exaltation of larks. What term would you use for groomsmen and bridesmaids? A band, a bevy, a gaggle?

The flower girl made her way down the aisle with the appropriate amount of adorableness, and then there was a Significant Pause.

The congregation rose to their feet and stood in respectful silence. The organist halted for a dramatic moment, fingers poised above the keys, before launching into "Ode to Joy."

And then, there she was: the lady of the hour.

Jessica Bullock.

There was an appreciative murmur from the crowd, and Ben couldn't blame them.

She was beautiful.

Her dress was elaborate and regal, and the jeweled tiara she wore added to the princess-like effect. Her hair was loose, rippling in soft golden waves over her bare shoulders. As she drew closer, Ben could see the familiar blue of her eyes, the color of a clear autumn sky.

The smile on her face was just right—sweet and a little bit shy, as befitted a blushing bride. Ben was sure everyone in this church was convinced she was as happy as she looked.

But he knew better.

With every step she took down the aisle, the disconnect between her appearance and her true emotions became more obvious to him. He felt like he was seeing two Jessicas: the one most people saw, and one very few could see.

The Jessica he saw wasn't glowing with bridal joy. She was numb, miserable, trapped.

Then she drew level with him, and their eyes met. Her façade was shaken—her facial muscles tensed, and her eyes widened for just a moment.

The moment was soon over. Now she was at the altar, being kissed by her father and handed off to Tom Shelburne.

But he wasn't interested in Tom. The only person he cared about was Jessica.

"Sit," his mother whispered, tugging on his jacket sleeve.

Only then did he notice that he was still standing while the rest of the wedding guests had taken their seats. He let himself sink back down, his eyes on his old friend.

At that moment that's what Jessica was. Not an estranged childhood companion, not someone he'd disliked in high school, not a person from his past he hadn't seen in years.

She was his old friend, and she was in trouble.

"I have to help her."

Only when his mother shushed him did he realize he'd spoken out loud.

He didn't say anything else. But as the ceremony continued, he knew he couldn't let this marriage happen.

He had to do something to stop it. But just as he was starting to stand, he heard a man's voice behind him.

"Tom."

Ben swiveled his head along with everyone else in the church.

Standing there in the aisle was a man Ben had never seen before. He was in his late thirties or early forties, with thinning dark hair and intense dark eyes.

The minister stopped talking. Jessica gasped, but after that there was dead silence. Everyone was staring at the stranger who was staring at Tom. It was obvious that as far as he was concerned, Tom was the only one there who mattered.

"It was harder when we met," the man said. He spoke quietly, but his words echoed in the silent church. "We live in a different world now. I'm not saying things will always be easy, but we don't have to be afraid of who we are. Not anymore." He took a step toward the altar. "And even if we did, I wouldn't give a damn. Life is short. Too short not to spend it with your soul mate."

He didn't say anything else. He just waited, holding Tom's gaze with his.

Ben could feel the stunned amazement all around him. Beside him, his mother gripped his arm.

But the only reaction he cared about was Jessica's.

Her face was pale, but not from surprise.

That was the reason for the tension behind her façade. She'd known Tom was gay. But then why had she been willing to go along with this charade? What the hell had she been thinking?

Standing beside her at the altar, Tom closed his eyes. "I love you," he whispered. Then he opened his eyes and said it again, loud enough to be heard all through the church. "I love you, Everett."

In the first pew on the groom's side, Tom's mother collapsed against his father.

Everett started to walk toward the altar, but Tom held up a hand. "Wait," he said, his voice shaking. Then he turned to his fiancée.

"Jessica, I . . . I don't know what to say. You're my best friend, and I'm hurting you worse than I've hurt anyone in my life. If you want to scream at me or curse me or punch me in the face, I deserve it."

When he stopped talking, he just stood there, waiting.

There was a long moment of silence. Then Jessica lifted her chin.

"There is something I'd like to say to you. Here in front of all our family and friends."

Tom braced himself and nodded. "Go ahead."

Her lower lip was trembling. "I'm so proud of you, Tom. And . . . and . . . I'm happy for you, too."

She pressed her lips together to stop the trembling, and then turned to address the church. "I guess it's obvious that the wedding is off. I'm so sorry that I . . . that we . . ." She took a deep breath. "I'm sorry. But I want to thank you all for coming. And the reception is paid for, so . . . I hope some of you will join me there. There'll be food . . . and music . . . and . . ."

The invitation seemed to use up Jessica's courage. As she looked out at the stunned congregation, her eyes filled with sudden tears.

The minister stepped forward then and spoke to her in a low voice. He led her away toward a small side door behind the altar, and her parents and sister hurried after her.

The moment the door closed behind them, the church erupted into shocked conversation. But Ben, who hadn't been able to stay still or silent when everyone else was, now found himself sitting like a stone.

Tom was gay. Jessica had known he was gay, and she'd agreed to marry him anyway.

And then it had blown up in her face in the most public way imaginable.

All during high school, Ben had half wished that something would blow up in Jessica's face. He'd hated the stereotype she'd turned herself into—the shallow rich girl obsessed with appearances and tearing other people down—and there'd been times he'd thought she'd be better off if someone or something humbled her, reminding her of her own days as an outsider.

Well, that wish had come true . . . ten years after the fact. And he felt sick.

On the other side of his mother, his father spoke up. "What in the hell just happened?"

His mother was shaking her head slowly. "I can't believe it. That poor, poor girl."

His father sighed. "Well, at least we don't have to go to the reception."

"I don't know," his mother said. "Maybe we ought to—"

Ben rose to his feet. "We're going to the reception."

His parents, still sitting, stared up at him.

"I practically had to drag you to this wedding," his mother said. "You've been acting like a fractious child all day. And now that you're off the hook, you want to go to the reception?"

"I, for one, absolutely refuse," his father put in. "These things are bad enough when the bride and groom actually get married."

"We're going," Ben said again.

His mother threw up her hands. "But *why?*"

"Jessica invited us." He gestured toward the altar. "Didn't you hear her?"

"Well, yes—but she was only being brave."

"Exactly. And we're going to support her."

~

The minister was talking, and her sister, too.

"Are you all right?"

"What can we do?"

No, I'm not all right. And there's nothing you can do.

Her parents were in the background, and—miracle of miracles—they weren't blaming her or criticizing her.

They were probably in shock.

Everyone in that church had been in shock. Her extended family, her friends, her parents' friends . . . staring at the train wreck happening in front of them, unable to look away.

But for some reason, only one face stood out in her memory.

Ben Taggart.

Months before, when she'd seen his name on her mother's invitation list, it had given her a jolt. They'd been friends once—good friends—but that had been during childhood and junior high, a time she'd worked hard to forget.

She'd cut him out of her life in high school. She'd been a bitch to him, in fact, which wasn't something she was proud of. She would have preferred not to have him at her wedding, but the Taggarts were old friends of her parents and she couldn't disinvite their son.

A while later she'd asked if Ben had RSVP'd, and her mother said he had. Then she'd asked if he was bringing a date, and her mother said no, he was coming stag.

She wasn't sure why she'd asked. What did it matter to her if Ben had a girlfriend? They hadn't even seen each other for a couple of years.

The last time they'd had a real conversation was in high school. It hadn't gone well.

She'd said something snide to another student and Ben had called her on it. He'd told her she was shallow and superficial. That she'd turned her back on her true friends and the only decent people in her life. That he didn't even recognize the person she'd become. That he'd love nothing more than to see her knocked off her high horse.

Boy, had his wish ever come true.

Ben Taggart had been there to see her humiliated. He'd been there to see the lies exposed, the shattering of the illusions she'd worked so hard to create.

"I'll kill him."

That was her father, muttering imprecations under his breath.

"What he did was unforgivable," her mother said, her voice trembling. "Did you see his parents? I don't think they'll ever speak to him again."

Tom. Oh, Tom.

Even though she was collateral damage in the explosion, she really was proud of him. To declare himself like that, in front of everybody, knowing that his own parents would judge and reject him—that had taken real courage.

All their lives, she and Tom had shared one defining characteristic: cowardice.

That was why they'd planned this sham marriage. They would shelter each other from the things they feared—shield each other from the world.

Now Tom had found his courage, and left her all alone.

She was proud of him. She was happy for him.

But that didn't stop her from being sad for herself.

Her parents were warming to their subject: vilifying Tom. Even Vicki, who usually tried to see everyone's side of a story, had joined in.

And suddenly, a path opened before her. Not a way to escape humiliation—there was no evading that—but of escaping her parents' disapproval.

She could let them blame Tom.

It wouldn't do him any additional injury. He wouldn't expect the parents of the woman he'd jilted to be his biggest fans.

But it would be a lie. And since she had nothing else to lose, she might as well speak the truth for once in her life.

"It wasn't Tom's fault."

That shut everybody up.

"I knew Tom was gay. I decided to marry him anyway."

Taking advantage of the stunned silence, she turned to Vicki and grabbed her hand. "Will you come with me back to the hotel? I have to change for the reception."

"You're not serious," her mother said. "You can't possibly—"

"I want to see the people who go," she said. "Because they'll be the people who care about me."

"Hardly," her mother snapped. "They'll be the people who want to see you writhing in embarrassment—and your family, too."

"You and Dad don't have to go."

Her mother stared at her, and she stared back. If a man of the cloth hadn't been there, Samantha Bullock would have had a lot more to say. But the minister's presence restrained her.

"Very well," she said, her voice iron-hard. "We won't."

Vicki gasped. "Mom—"

"We'll see you both tomorrow," her mother said.

And with that, Samantha and William Bullock made their exit.

Vicki started to sputter in indignation, but Jessica stopped her. "It's okay," she said. "It'll be easier without them there."

Her sister looked worried. "Are you sure you want to do this?"

She'd told a church full of people she'd be at the reception, and for once in her life she wasn't going to be a coward.

"I'm sure."

CHAPTER THREE

The room looked beautiful.

As Jessica stood in the doorway and surveyed the scene, she felt an odd sense of detachment . . . almost as though she were a guest at someone else's wedding.

Every detail was flawless. It all looked exactly as she had envisioned, and for a control freak, there could be no sweeter triumph.

If only she'd been the wedding planner instead of the bride. Then, at least, she could take some professional satisfaction in the planning and aesthetic instinct that had led to this moment of event-planning perfection.

Unfortunately, she was the bride. The jilted bride, she reminded herself, fighting the urge to turn and flee.

At least she wasn't wearing her wedding gown anymore. She'd changed into the blue silk dress she'd planned to wear tomorrow, when she and Tom were supposed to leave for their honeymoon.

Once people saw her standing there, it was too late to run. She stiffened her spine, lifted her chin, and took a deep breath.

There were a surprising number of people here, all things considered. Had they come to jeer, as her mother had implied?

The first wave of guests reached her. She searched their faces, but there was no mockery or satisfied malice in anyone's eyes. All she saw was kindness, warmth, and sympathy.

Would she have been so compassionate to someone else in her position? Or would she have derided them from behind the defensive fortress she'd spent so many years constructing?

That fortress was gone now. It lay in ruins all around her, exposing . . . what?

That was the danger in hiding behind walls for so long. Eventually, the walls became more real than whatever was behind them. Now that the walls had been destroyed, what remained?

She had a horrible feeling that the answer was nothing.

But she didn't have to ask that question right now. Now she had something else to face: all the people who'd actually shown up at what had become a sideshow instead of a wedding reception, with herself as the main attraction.

The first person to reach her was Simone, which helped. Simone's sturdy friendship and I-don't-give-a-crap attitude was like a drink of cool water on a hot day. With Simone on her right and Vicki on her left, she might actually get through the next hour.

Then she saw Ben Taggart across the room.

Their eyes locked and Jessica felt a hot rush of embarrassment. Why did it bother her so much that he'd witnessed her humiliation? Hundreds of other people had, too—and almost all of them were a bigger part of her current life than Ben was.

Maybe it was because Ben had always been so honest himself, and so impatient with anything like artifice. In that brief moment when their eyes had met in church, he'd given her the same feeling he always had: that he was seeing below the surface.

The other guests had been smiling and happy for her—all the things you'd expect. But Ben had been frowning. Not in disapproval, exactly, but in . . . recognition? Concern?

She wasn't sure what he'd been feeling. But he'd figured out what no one else but Simone had—that something was wrong. That the smiling face she wore walking down that aisle was a mask.

Now he was here, at the reception. Why? Was he reveling in her humiliation? That would be a little petty, considering that any grudge he might have against her was fifteen years old. Had he come because he felt sorry for her? That would be a hundred times worse.

A knot of people had drifted between her and Ben, obscuring her view of him. Now the crowd shifted and she got a clearer look.

He looked good, was the first unbidden thought that came to her mind. He shouldn't, because he hated suits and he ought to look stiff as a board in one. But even though he'd always looked better in jeans and T-shirts, he looked good in suits, too.

He looked good in everything. He always had.

His dark hair was a bit longer than she usually liked on men, but it suited him. That, along with the lean power of his body and the rough, masculine planes of his face, made a fascinating contrast with the subdued lines of his jacket and tie.

And then, in a flashback to adolescence, her body responded with an electric rush that raised goose bumps on her skin.

They hadn't seen each other in years and she was right in the middle of the worst day of her life, but apparently her hormones still clung to out-of-date programming.

But she'd been able to hide her reactions back then, when she was just a kid. She could certainly hide them now.

Especially if she didn't get any closer. If there was any social function in the world at which she could abandon Emily Post's rules of etiquette, surely this was it. She wasn't going to "graciously greet all her guests," damn it—especially when it came to Ben.

"I don't know about you, but I think this occasion calls for hard liquor," Simone said.

"I agree," Vicki put in immediately. "In fact, that's the best idea I've heard all day."

Kate Meredith, Jessica's other college roommate and Simone's best friend, grabbed her hand.

"What do you say, Jess? Do you want to get drunk?"

She hadn't been drunk since college. She started to say no, but the bar was on the side of the room farthest from Ben.

"Yes. Yes, I do."

The band started playing a few minutes later. As people got up to dance with more abandon than you usually saw at a wedding reception, the crowd of people around Jessica thinned out until it was down to Kate, Simone, Vicki, and her other bridesmaids, who were clustered around her at the bar and matching her shot for shot.

"What is this called again?" she asked as she downed her fourth without coughing, an achievement she was unexpectedly proud of.

"Jägermeister."

"Why does it taste so much better now than it did half an hour ago?"

Simone tossed down her own shot. "That's the Jäger therapy kicking in. It makes everything go down easier."

"Even getting left at the altar by your gay fiancé?"

Simone grinned at her. "Even that."

The band started a song Jessica didn't know, and Simone burst out laughing. "Who requested this? What a genius choice."

Jessica listened until the song reached its two-word chorus: "Love *Stinks*!"

For just a moment she was horrified. Then, as the song went on, she started to giggle.

If someone had told her an hour ago that she'd actually be laughing at this reception, she'd have thought they were crazy.

"Thank you," she said suddenly, looking around at the bridesmaids who hadn't left her side since she'd entered the room.

"For what?" Kate asked.

"For being here. For getting me drunk. For putting up with me for the last year. For everything."

Before she knew what was happening, the breath was being squeezed out of her in a group hug.

"Whoa. Okay, I need to breathe," she said.

Then she heard an older female voice.

"Jessica?"

As her bridesmaids gave her space, she saw Ben's mother standing there. Her husband was with her, but not, she was relieved to see, her son.

Amelia Taggart smiled and took her hand. "We're leaving now, but we wanted to thank you for inviting us. Seth says it's the most fun he's ever had at a wedding reception."

"Good food and good music, just like you promised," he said.

Jessica had always liked the Taggarts. "The afternoon didn't go quite the way I planned, but I'm very glad you came. Thank you."

"It was our pleasure," Amelia said. She hesitated a moment, and then she gathered Jessica in her arms for a hug. "If there's ever anything we can do . . ."

"I'll let you know."

As soon as they were gone she looked around for Ben. Had he left before his parents? Or was he still here somewhere?

Scanning the room for him, she was struck again by how much fun people were having. The liquor was flowing at the tables as well as here at the bar. People were dancing, talking, eating, laughing.

It had turned out to be a pretty good party.

But as she watched her guests enjoying themselves, a wave of depression brought her own alcohol-inflated mood back down to earth. After all this was over, she would go to the apartment she and Tom were supposed to share . . . except that she would be alone.

Even here, surrounded by all these people—including some who were better friends than she'd given them credit for—she felt alone.

The bartender set her fifth shot on the mahogany bar. But as she started to reach for it, she finally caught sight of Ben. He was making his way through the crowd, but not toward the doors.

He was coming toward her.

Oh God. What did he want? To rub her nose in her humiliation, or to say something kind?

She honestly didn't know which she'd hate more.

She left the shot on the bar, muttered something about needing the restroom, and fled.

The hallway outside the reception hall wasn't very crowded. She really did need a bathroom, so she was glad to see the sign across the hall.

She was sitting on the toilet when she heard the outer door open. Two college-aged girls were chattering together as they came into the restroom, and she recognized their voices, although she didn't know them well. They were cousins on her father's side.

"Someone started a hashtag on Twitter. #JessicaWeddingFail. Have you seen it? It's hysterical. I tweeted out the picture I took of her standing alone at the altar."

"Oh my God, classic. That dress probably cost twenty thousand dollars. And the wedding had to be at least a hundred thousand. Can you imagine spending that much money just to tell the world you're a fag hag? She's been lording it over everyone for, like, years, and now Tom dumps her at the altar—for a *man*."

They must have come in for a quick makeup check, because they left without using the facilities. Once the door closed behind them the bathroom was silent.

Jessica stayed where she was for a minute. Then she left the stall and went to the sink, turning on the faucet with shaking hands.

This was what her mother had warned her would happen. This was what her friends had shielded her from, at least for the last hour.

Almost every decision she'd made for the last fifteen years had been to protect herself from feeling vulnerable. All she'd ever wanted was to feel safe, strong, unassailable. She and Tom had decided to get married for the same reason—so they could help each other hide from the judgment of the world.

Now all that had been undone. She was exposed, weak, defenseless.

Not since eighth grade when the "mean girls" had bullied her for being a fat loser had she felt so powerless. Ben had told her over and over again that it didn't matter, that she was better than all the kids who tried to tear her down, that he'd be her friend no matter what.

But the summer before ninth grade, she'd turned her back on Ben in order to forge a new path for herself. Two things had happened that summer: her uncle Jeffrey had moved out of the city, and her parents had offered to send her to a fat farm.

Her uncle's leaving had put an end to something she'd never told another living soul—not her parents and not Ben. Once Jeffrey was gone, she'd decided to put the ugliness behind her. It would be as though it had never happened. She had a chance to start over, to remake herself—starting with her physical appearance.

By the time that summer was over, she saw a new future unfolding. She would never again be a victim, never again be on the outside, vulnerable and exposed. She would be on the inside, where it was safe. She would be popular, she would be beautiful, and she would never let anyone see her soft underbelly ever again.

Her plan had succeeded. And when her uncle passed away a few years later, it had seemed as though that part of her life was behind her for good.

Jessica turned off the faucet and leaned on the bathroom counter, staring at herself in the mirror. The one promise she'd made to her teenage self was that she'd never be anyone's fool. Now, here she was—everyone's fool.

She was a punch line. A hashtag. And as grateful as she was to Vicki and to her friends for standing by her today, they couldn't change that. For the rest of her life, she would be known as the Park Avenue bride who'd been dumped at the altar. The socialite whose fiancé had left her for another man. Whenever she walked into a room, what had happened today would be the first thing—maybe the only thing—that anyone remembered about her.

It would follow her forever.

At the age of fourteen, she'd decided to reshape her life. She'd done everything she could to make a total break with the person she'd been, and she'd succeeded.

At twenty-eight, that option was no longer viable. In the age of social media there would be no escape, no burying of the past. There would be no place to hide.

But she could at least hide tonight. She could turn off her phone and leave this reception.

She wouldn't even go back to the hall to say goodbye. She was sure her friends would forgive her for that, and no one else would blame her.

But when she emerged from the bathroom, she saw one obstacle to her plan. Ben Taggart, his back to her, was standing between her and the hotel exit.

Her heart leapt into her throat. Afraid he would turn and see her, she ducked into an empty function room.

There must have been an event in here not long before. There were coffee urns on one side of the room and cups scattered around the empty tables. Jessica sat down at one of them, put her elbows on the table, and covered her face with her hands.

~

Ben turned in time to see Jessica disappear into an empty room.

He went to the doorway and looked inside. Jessica was sitting with her back to him, her shoulders slumped and her head in her hands.

He should probably leave her alone. That was obviously what she wanted, and if he left now, he could catch the beginning of the Mets game at O'Malley's.

But she looked so fragile and forlorn that his heart tightened in his chest.

He moved into the room and took a chair next to her.

"Hey, Jess," he said gently.

When she raised her head he could see she'd been crying. Her face was streaked with tears and her eyes were red-rimmed, and the sight tore at his heart.

She took a deep breath and straightened her spine. "Are you here to gloat? I know seeing me humiliated is a dream come true for you."

Her lips were trembling, and she looked so defensive he wondered if it had been a mistake to follow her in here.

"I wanted to make sure you're all right. And I wanted to tell you how proud I am of you."

She stared at him. "Proud of me?"

"For standing by Tom. For saying what you did to him. That took guts, Jess. So did coming to this reception." He paused. "It's been a hell of a day. How are you doing?"

There was a flash of anger in her blue eyes.

"Well, let's see. I walked down the aisle in front of everyone I know and got left at the altar by my gay fiancé. How do you think I'm doing?"

That made him smile. "If you're snapping at me, you're doing better than I thought."

She frowned. "What does that mean?"

"When you were in that church, you looked numb. Like you were standing outside yourself, watching things happen to you. You looked like you'd given up. But if you can muster up the energy to be pissed at me, it means you're still fighting."

She shook her head slowly. "Fighting for what?"

"For yourself. For your happiness. That's worth fighting for, Jess."

She looked down at the table, a furrow drawing her brows together.

After a moment she looked up again. "Why did you come to the wedding? It's not like we're friends. You could have declined the invitation."

"You want the truth?"

She shrugged. "When have you ever bothered to lie about anything?"

"My mother made me."

For the first time, her mouth curved up in a smile.

"She did, huh? That sounds like Amelia."

They were both quiet after that. This was probably a good time for him to leave—he'd said what he wanted to say, and he'd gotten her to smile. He should quit while he was ahead.

"What's next for you?" he asked.

She blinked at him. "Next? What do you mean?"

"What happens tomorrow? What happens the next day?"

She shrugged. "I don't know."

"Well, what *was* going to happen? If you and Tom had gotten married, what were you going to do next?"

He'd hated the numbness he'd seen in her at the altar—the mechanical way she'd moved and spoken. He wanted to know that Jessica had something to look forward to, some purpose for her life outside of getting married.

That's what he'd been getting at when he'd asked her what was next. But the answer she gave was, "Our honeymoon."

Okay, fine. He could start there.

"The honeymoon. Where were you going?"

She sighed. "Bermuda."

He was surprised. "Bermuda? Seriously?"

That seemed to put her back up a little. "What's wrong with Bermuda?"

He held out his hands. "Nothing. Not a thing. I just figured you and Tom would go to Europe or something. Bermuda seems . . ." He trailed off when he saw her glaring at him. "Sorry," he said quickly. "Bermuda is great. What made you want to go there? Was it Tom's idea?"

"No. It was mine." She lifted her shoulders and let them fall. "They have this dolphin program."

He wasn't sure he'd heard her right. "Dolphin program?"

She looked a little embarrassed. "I've always had this thing for dolphins."

He had a sudden memory of her room in eighth grade. "My God, yes. You had all those dolphin books and posters and that charm necklace . . ."

"Right," she went on quickly, her cheeks turning pink. "So . . . Bermuda has this program. It's called 'A Day with Dolphins.' You spend time in their habitat, swimming with them and learning from the trainers how to take care of them and work with them and . . . and . . ." She trailed off at the expression on Ben's face. "I suppose that seems stupid to you."

It didn't seem stupid at all. This was the first time in fifteen years he'd gotten a glimpse of the girl Jessica had once been.

"No, it doesn't," he said. "It seems wonderful. I think you should go."

She stared at him in disbelief. "On my honeymoon? Alone?" She rolled her eyes. "Sure, that'll cheer me up."

The more he thought about it, the more he liked the idea. "Why the hell not? It's not like you were going to get laid even if Tom had been there."

She glared at him. "That's a low blow."

He grinned. "Too soon to joke about it?"

"Yes."

"Okay, fine. But why shouldn't you go? The trip's paid for, isn't it? And you can do your dolphin thing."

She started to say no. But then she stopped, and he could see that she was actually thinking about it.

"You can't tell me it wouldn't be nice," he said persuasively. "A week by yourself on an island, away from New York?"

Her mouth twisted wryly. "Away from daily reminders of my humiliation, you mean? Bermuda's not far enough for that. Twitter makes embarrassment a global event. Do you know there's a hashtag about me? #JessicaWeddingFail. Apparently one of my cousins live-tweeted the ceremony."

"Well, then, your cousin's an asshole. But who cares what anyone else says about you? That's not what this would be about. This would be about taking some time for yourself, to figure things out. And to swim with dolphins," he added.

She looked torn. Then:

"I couldn't go on my honeymoon alone. That's the most pathetic thing I've ever heard. I can't possibly—"

"Jessica."

"What?"

"Answer me this. When you say it's pathetic, are you thinking about what other people might think, or what you think yourself?"

"Both." She paused. "Okay, other people," she went on grudgingly.

"That's what I thought. Listen, Jess—if there was ever a time in your life to not give a damn about what other people think, this is it. And you really want to do that dolphin program. Don't you? When's the last time you did something just because you wanted to do it?"

A sudden spasm went over her face. "I'm a rich socialite living in Manhattan. Doesn't that mean I always do what I want to do? Don't you think my life is an endless series of indulgences?"

"No," he said. "I don't. Do you want to know what I really think?"

She looked a little wary. "Okay."

"I think you've always had everything except the things you really want."

Her eyes filled with sudden tears. She looked away, blinking, and took a deep breath.

"Go to Bermuda," he said softly. "Do it for yourself."

"I can't stay alone in a honeymoon suite. I can't. I—"

"Get a different room."

She shook her head. "The hotel's full. All the good places are booked up. There's a yacht race and some big cricket match going on."

"Take a friend, then."

She shook her head again. "The plane leaves tomorrow morning. Who would drop everything to come with me on the most pathetic vacation ever?"

"Your sister."

"She's on call at the hospital."

"One of your bridesmaids."

"None of them could take ten days off with no notice. They're not teachers like you, Ben. They don't get summers off."

Teachers like you.

Her words gave him a crazy idea—an idea he might not have considered if he hadn't had a couple of scotches at the reception.

"I don't have the summer off, but I have the rest of this month off." After that he'd be getting ready for his move to Chicago, but he was a free agent until then.

She raised her eyebrows. "That's nice, but not relevant. Unless you're offering to come to Bermuda with me?"

Her tone of voice made it obvious that she was joking—and that she thought he was, too.

For one brief moment the sober, reasonable voices in his head shouted at him not to be a lunatic. But when he spoke, it wasn't those voices that won the day.

"Yeah," he said. "I am."

Jessica stared at him. "What?"

He had a sensation of having stepped over the edge of a cliff, but since it was too late to back up he might as well go with it.

"Why not? As you pointed out, I'm a teacher—and the school year's over." Suddenly he grinned. "I mean, hell. It's all paid for, right? I'd be getting a free trip to Bermuda."

She looked at him like he was crazy—or like she was waiting for him to say she was being punked. "You realize we'd be sharing a honeymoon suite for ten days?"

"On a platonic basis, obviously. If I was looking for a date, there are easier ways to go about it."

"Where are you planning to sleep?"

"It's a suite, right? I'm sure there'll be a couch for me. Maybe it'll even fold out."

"You couldn't use Tom's plane ticket. It's nontransferable."

Ben reached into his inside jacket pocket and pulled out his smartphone. "What airline are you going on?"

She told him. "But I don't remember the flight number."

"I'll find it. What time does the plane leave?"

"Eight fifteen."

His fingers moved quickly over the screen. After a minute he looked up. "The flight's not sold out," he said. "I can buy a ticket right now."

She stared at him, and he stared back.

"You're not serious," she said finally.

"Yeah? Let's find out. Say the word, Jess, and I'm on that plane."

"You don't really mean it. You'd back out if I said yes."

He put the phone on the table between them, his index finger poised over the screen. "There's one sure way to find out. Say the word and I'll do it."

She leaned back in her chair and folded her arms. "Go ahead, then. Do it."

He held her gaze for a moment, a sudden grin lighting his face. Then his eyes flicked down to the phone as his fingers tapped busily.

He slid the phone back into his pocket and then mirrored her position, sitting back in his chair with his arms folded.

But while she was staring at him in dawning horror, he was still grinning.

"It's done," he said. "Pink sand beaches, here I come."

The implications of what had just happened seemed to sweep over her. "Undo it!"

He shook his head. "Nope. It's been years since I've taken a real vacation. This will do me good." He clasped his hands behind his head, gazing up at the ceiling. "It'll be awesome. Lazing by the beach, drinking rum, watching you swim with dolphins—"

"Shut up and call that damn airline. They'll refund your money if you—"

"No, they won't. They have a very strict policy about—"

"Then I'll pay you back. How much was the ticket? I'll write you a check as soon as I—"

"Jessica." His teasing tone turned serious, and he rested his hands on his knees as he leaned forward. "Life is short, and you've

35

already spent too much of yours doing things other people thought you should do. For once, do something because *you* want to. Because you'll enjoy it. I'll be there in case you want company, but if you'd rather pretend I don't exist, that's fine with me."

She made a face without realizing it, and Ben burst out laughing. "Okay, maybe I'm not great at being invisible. But I swear to God, Jess—if you go on this trip, I'll do my best not to piss you off too much. How's that for an offer?"

She got up from her chair, pacing slowly around the room. Ben sat back and waited for her decision. He'd made his best case, and it was up to her now.

After a minute she came back and sat down again. Her eyes searched his face, and he wondered what she was looking for.

Whatever it was, she must have found it. "Okay," she said.

Ben raised an eyebrow. "You mean it?"

"Yes. But I was left at the altar today, and I have four shots of Jägermeister in my system. I'm probably not in my right mind." She frowned at him. "How much have you had to drink?"

He grinned at her. "A scotch or two."

"Are you in your right mind?"

"It's too soon to say." He rose to his feet. "I guess I'd better go home and pack. I've got a plane to catch tomorrow morning."

CHAPTER FOUR

When the alarm went off the next morning, Ben resisted the urge to hurl his phone across the room. Instead, he silenced the beeping and closed his eyes again.

He must have set the alarm by mistake. The school year was over, and this was his sleeping-in season.

He wasn't a morning person, which was one of the many ironies inherent in his chosen career. He usually guarded his weekend and summer mornings jealously, never scheduling anything before ten if he could help it.

He'd just fallen back asleep when the phone started making noises again.

This time it wasn't the alarm, though. Someone was calling him.

Who the hell was calling him at five in the morning?

He grabbed his phone and stared at the screen.

Jessica.

In a rush it all came back. His offer to go with her to Bermuda, made in a fit of insanity. His impulsive purchase of an overpriced last-minute plane ticket, made with a credit card he'd designated "for emergencies only." Their exchange of phone numbers before he left the hotel.

Please, God, let her be calling to cancel this trip . . . or to tell him not to go.

He hit Accept. "Hey."

"It's Jessica," she said briskly.

No one should sound that brisk this early in the morning.

"I know."

"I wanted to be sure you were up, and to remind you not to forget your passport. We should be there in twenty minutes."

"We?"

"The driver and I. I told you last night we'd pick you up at five thirty. Don't you remember?"

Barely.

"Yeah, of course."

He closed his eyes. So this was really happening. He and Jessica were going to Bermuda together. For ten days.

There was a pause, and he wondered if his network had dropped the call. Then:

"Unless you've changed your mind," she said.

He opened his eyes again, frowning up at the ceiling. Was she hoping he'd changed his mind?

Well, why not? He'd been hoping she'd changed her mind.

"Why are you asking me that?" he asked cautiously.

"Well." She cleared her throat. "I had some time to think last night, and you were right. Definitely. You were definitely right, about this trip being good for me and something I should, you know, definitely do. For myself." Pause. "But there's no need for you to come with me," she went on. "I mean, I know you offered to make sure I would go, and mission accomplished. I'm going. But there's certainly no reason for you to throw your life into disarray. I know school is out, but I'm sure you've got other obligations and commitments. And let's be honest. We're not really friends, and we haven't seen each other in years. So . . ." She paused again. "So, you can say bon voyage to me and go back to your life. I'd like to pay you back for the ticket, but of course I can't force you to take the money. I could send a check to your favorite charity if you'd prefer. If you don't want to go, that is. Which you probably don't. Of course you're still welcome to go, if . . ." She trailed off. "If you still want to," she finished.

Silence.

All during her little speech, Ben had been thinking that this was the perfect out. He'd convinced her to take the trip, which really had been his goal. But she was right: they weren't friends anymore, and they hadn't seen each other in years, and there was no guarantee they'd even be able to carry on a conversation. Now that she was prepared to go to Bermuda by herself, was there any need for him to go, too?

No, there wasn't.

No need at all.

But as he thought that, an image flashed into his mind—Jessica sitting slumped in that empty function room, with tear-stained cheeks and red-rimmed eyes. She'd been raw and vulnerable in a way he hadn't seen in a long time.

He couldn't see her right now, but of course she would have erased all traces of yesterday's emotion. He could visualize her sitting straight in the backseat of her limo, clothes and makeup flawless and every hair in place.

Her mask was back in place, too. He could hear it in her voice.

How would she react if he decided not to go? She might be relieved; she might be disappointed. Maybe she'd be a little of both. Now that she'd reverted to perfectly-in-control Jessica, it would be hard to tell what she was feeling.

But he'd made the offer last night because she was hurting and he wanted to help. Maybe they weren't friends now, maybe they hadn't been in years, but seeing Jessica in pain had torn at something inside him.

For better or worse, he was going to follow that instinct. He wouldn't let her go on this trip alone.

"No way," he said. "I've never been to Bermuda, and I'm not missing this chance."

"But—"

"No buts. I'll see you in twenty minutes."

There was a short silence. "Well . . . all right. Don't forget your passport."

He smiled at the ceiling. "I won't."

~

Jessica glanced at her watch. There was an hour to go before they landed.

Ben had bought a coach ticket, but when Jessica had explained their situation to the crew—the first and last time, she decided, that she would play the jilted fiancée card—a sympathetic flight attendant had let Ben use Tom's seat.

The first-class section was only half full, and the seats nearest theirs were empty. There was plenty of privacy for conversation, but so far they hadn't taken advantage of it.

Ben was in the aisle seat perusing the *New York Times*. She had a magazine open on her lap, but she wasn't reading it.

She wanted to fidget, but she controlled herself. She'd spent years disciplining her behavior in public, and it was so automatic now that she suppressed the urge to shift in her seat almost before she noticed it was there.

She used to have all kinds of bad habits—twisting her hair, biting her nails, emotional eating. But she'd managed to eliminate them all.

Ben Taggart hadn't been a bad habit. He'd been a friend—maybe her best friend. But once she'd begun her relentless pursuit of perfection and popularity, Ben was an uncomfortable reminder of the life she'd wanted to put behind her. The good and the bad were tangled up together and she'd made a cold-blooded decision to cut it all away.

She hadn't been able to think of a way to explain that, so she hadn't even tried. She'd just turned her back on him and trusted that he would get the hint.

He had, of course. But that hadn't stopped him from voicing his opinion on the new-and-improved Jessica every so often.

Every time he'd accused her of being superficial, she'd resented it. Not because he was wrong—she'd be the first to admit that she focused on superficial things in high school—but because he didn't understand that she was just doing her best to survive in a difficult world.

He didn't understand that because of who he was. Ben Taggart had never been afraid of difficulty or struggle or pain . . . or anything else.

While she tried hard to fit in, he boldly stood out. When she agreed with a prevailing opinion, he went out of his way to be the voice of dissent. While she took the smooth path whenever she could, he marched cheerfully into the jungle with a machete, clearing away obstacles with the force of his personality.

She remembered the drama around Ben's college education, when her parents and everyone in their circle had been abuzz with the Taggarts' situation. Seth and Amelia had told their son that if he insisted on becoming a public school teacher, they wouldn't pay his tuition. He'd be on his own.

He'd accepted that challenge without hesitation, taking out student loans and holding down three jobs to pay his way at a community college. After a year his parents had backed down, declaring they were proud that Ben had stuck to his guns and supporting his transfer to a four-year university with a renowned education department.

But not everyone could be like Ben and survive. Not everyone could—

"What are you thinking about?"

She turned her head, startled. "What?"

Ben had put down his newspaper and was leaning back in his seat, a quizzical look on his face.

"You were frowning just now, like you were arguing with someone in your head. I wondered what you were thinking about."

He looked relaxed and comfortable in jeans and a Mets T-shirt, while she was dressed in an ivory linen pantsuit that would wrinkle if you looked at it wrong. Luckily her unique set of life skills included not wrinkling her clothes.

"I wasn't thinking about anything in particular," she said.

"That's too bad."

He was smiling at her, which made his brown eyes look warm and full of life. She resisted the urge to smile back.

"Why is that too bad?"

"Because if you were arguing with someone in your head, you could tell me about it, and then we could have a conversation. As opposed to, you know, sitting here in silence."

She frowned. "I'm perfectly willing to have a conversation. We were sitting in silence because you were reading the newspaper."

"I was reading the newspaper because you pulled out a magazine the minute we sat down."

Okay, that was true.

"Well, I'm not reading now," she said. "What do you want to talk about?"

"We can talk about anything."

"All right, then. Were there any interesting articles in the *Times*?"

He shook his head. "When I said we could talk about anything, I didn't mean current events. I meant anything about our actual lives."

That didn't sound appealing. "I don't want to talk about my life. I'm going to Bermuda to get away from my life."

"You don't have to talk about Tom or the wedding or any of that. But you and I haven't had a real conversation in a long time. I don't know who you are now, and I'd like to. Especially since we're going on a ten-day vacation together."

She supposed that was reasonable. The only problem was, she wasn't sure who she was anymore. But she couldn't say that to Ben, who wouldn't understand. He'd always known exactly who he was.

"I don't know where to start," she said. "I mean . . . what do you want to know?"

"Do you still like the Backstreet Boys?"

That made her smile. "Of course not."

"Well, that was the last solid piece of information I had on your musical taste. What do you listen to these days?"

She shrugged. "Tom likes jazz, so I've been listening to a lot of that."

"Jazz, huh? Who are your favorite artists?"

She started to name some of Tom's favorites—Chet Baker and Miles Davis and Charlie Parker. But then she stopped.

"What is it?" Ben asked.

For some reason, she was remembering what he had said yesterday.

Life is short, and you've already spent too much of yours doing things other people thought you should do. For once, do something because you want to. Because you'll enjoy it.

"Nothing. I mean . . . if you're really interested in the music I like . . . the truth is, I don't really enjoy jazz. I only listened to it because Tom likes it."

She braced herself for Ben to say something critical. Something like, *Why did you waste your time listening to music you don't enjoy because your fake fiancé liked it?*

But he didn't. He just said, "Well, then, there's a perk to not marrying the guy. You'll never have to play another jazz song if you don't want to."

She smiled a little. "I guess that's true." She paused. "You know something else? I'll never have to watch another episode of *Murder, She Wrote.*"

"Tom's a fan?"

"Unfortunately, yes. It's his comfort show. Do you know it ran for twelve seasons? Two hundred and sixty-four episodes."

"That's a lot of murder."

She nodded. "Yes, it is. Jessica Fletcher is a menace to society. You know she lives in a tiny village in Maine? I don't know how anyone's left in that town. Everyone she knows has either been murdered, or is in jail for murder, or has been falsely accused of murder."

Ben laughed. "Okay, so you don't like *Murder, She Wrote.* What shows *do* you like?"

She thought about it. In high school and college, she'd watched whatever the cool kids were watching. Back home after that, her parents had mostly controlled the remote. Once she and Tom were living together, she let him choose whatever they were going to watch in the evenings. That usually meant a crime drama or a cable news show—neither of which she enjoyed.

She shrugged. "I don't know. I guess I'm not a big TV fan."

"What if you were on a desert island and had to pick one thing to watch?"

"Animal Planet, I guess. Or the National Geographic channel." Did that sound weird or boring? Probably both. "What about you?" she asked, wanting to change the subject. "What shows do you like?"

"Sports and sci-fi."

That made her smile. "So that hasn't changed, huh?"

"Nope. Do you remember when I made you watch that *Star Trek* marathon?"

"Please don't remind me."

"But you got me back. You made me sit through those old episodes of *The Undersea World of Jacques Cousteau*."

She covered her face with her hands. "Oh my God. Did I really?"

"Yep. But don't feel bad. I actually enjoyed it."

She let her hands fall back to her sides. "You did not."

"Sure I did." He looked thoughtful for a moment. "In junior high you said you were going to major in marine biology. Remember?"

She'd put that dream aside a long time ago. "Yes."

"What did you end up majoring in?"

"Business."

He stared at her. "You did?"

His expression made her feel defensive. "It was what my parents suggested, and they were paying the bills."

"Okay," he said after a moment. "So you majored in business. What did you do with your degree?"

Now she was feeling even more defensive. "I worked for my mother after I graduated. She sits on the boards of several organizations, and I helped her with event planning and fund-raising and things like that."

"You don't do that anymore?"

"I stopped once Tom and I got engaged. I was busy renovating our new apartment, and planning the wedding was a full-time job in itself."

Ben nodded, his expression neutral.

"What?" she demanded.

"What do you mean, what?"

"It's obvious that you're thinking something. What is it?"

He shook his head. "Nothing you need to get upset about. I was just wondering if part of the reason you got engaged to Tom was to get away from your parents."

She started to deny it—but then she found herself wondering, too.

She'd moved back home after she graduated from college, since there was plenty of room in her parents' place. They'd even converted a guest bedroom into a home office for her, making it easier for her to assist with her mother's work.

How had she felt when Tom had first suggested that the two of them get married? When she'd moved into his apartment after their engagement was official, and after that, when they'd gone apartment hunting together?

Relieved.

"Maybe," she said, looking down at her lap. Her legs were crossed, and her hands, primly folded, rested on her knee. Her linen suit was still unwrinkled.

"Hey, Jess?"

She looked up again and met Ben's eyes. "What?"

"I'm not trying to criticize you or make you feel bad. I'm honestly interested."

"Interested in what?"

"In you. In who you are now."

"I don't know who I am."

The words came out before she could censor them. Her face flushed and she turned away from Ben to look out the window.

She grew more and more tense as she waited for him to say something. To ask what she meant. When he did ask a question, though, it wasn't the one she'd expected.

"Why did you and Tom get engaged?"

Jessica looked back at him. "I thought you said we didn't have to talk about that."

"We don't have to. I just thought you might want to." He paused. "But it's up to you."

Her eyes searched his for a moment. Then she shrugged. "You won't like the answer."

"Why not?"

"Because you always want people to be brave. You want people to be honest. Don't you?"

"Sure. But I'm not an idiot, Jess. I know things get complicated. I know things aren't always black-and-white."

She looked down at her hands. "I don't think it would help to talk about it. I just want to put it behind me."

"You could do that. Or you could think of this trip as your chance to tell the truth without any repercussions. You can spend ten days telling me any damn thing you want, and it won't matter. I'll never say a word about it. Hell, once we get back to New York we probably won't even see each other again. So what do you have to lose?"

Maybe Ben was right. Would it really be so terrible to talk about it? She could get it out in the open, and then they could let it go for the rest of the trip.

She shrugged. "Tom and I have been friends for years. I've known he was gay since high school, but he didn't want anyone else to find out—especially his parents, who are really conservative. He was afraid it would affect his job, too. He's a trader and he works in a hyper-alpha-male atmosphere. So he stayed in the closet, but he was sick of family and friends asking him who he was dating and when he was getting married. I was, too. So we decided to help each other out. That's it."

He stared at her. "That's it? But what about—well, everything? What if you fell in love with somebody? Or hell, what if you just wanted to date somebody?"

She frowned. "If I answer that honestly, you won't believe me."

"Try me anyway."

She took a deep breath. "It wasn't an issue. I don't want to date, and I don't want to fall in love. I just want to be left alone."

She said those last words almost fiercely.

"But if you want to be left alone, why not just be alone? Why marry someone you don't love?"

"Just be alone, huh? Do you really think it's that easy?"

"Well, yeah. Why isn't it that easy?"

"Because we can't all be you, Ben. We're not all rugged individualists. We can't all thumb our noses at our families and people's expectations. Believe it or not, I didn't want to disappoint my family. And I didn't want to answer the same questions over and over, either. *Are you dating anyone? Is it serious? Do you think you'll get married soon?*"

"But—"

"I know, I know. What does it matter what other people think? Well, it matters to me. It always has and it probably always will. And the fact that you don't understand that doesn't make it any less true. I know that's anathema to you and I know you despise me because of it, but that doesn't change who I am."

Her lips trembled, and she pressed them firmly together. Then she turned her head and stared out the window.

"I don't despise you, Jess."

She swiveled her head to look him in the eyes. "That's not what you said in high school."

"You mean ten years ago? I hope I've changed a little since then."

She looked at him seriously. "But you haven't." She hurried on. "I don't mean that as a criticism. I just mean you're still doing what you think is right, no matter what anyone else thinks. You wanted to be a teacher when we were kids, and you are a teacher. You wanted to move away from the Upper East Side, and you did. You've done everything you said you would do."

He cocked his head to the side. "If I heard that from anyone but you, I'd assume it was a compliment. But since it was from you, I'm not sure what to think."

"I'm not complimenting you or criticizing you. I'm just stating a fact. You're the same person you were in high school."

"Just because I'm doing the job I wanted to do back then doesn't mean I'm the same person."

"So what's your point?"

"My point," he said patiently, "is that I don't hate you—even if I did back then." He paused. "And honestly? I don't think I did back then, either. But that's all in the past . . . along with your engagement. You have a chance to start a new phase of your life, Jess. That's kind of exciting if you think about it."

"To someone like you, maybe. But I'm not adventurous. I don't like uncertainty. I have no idea what the next phase of my life will look like, and that scares me."

Would she go crawling back to her parents? Ask them to give her a home and a job again? Or would she live by herself and get a job on her own?

She sighed. "I don't want to think about the future right now. This trip is supposed to be my escape from all that, at least for a while."

"Fair enough. But can I ask you one more thing?"

"I guess it depends on what it is."

"Why don't you want to date or fall in love?"

She might have been willing to tell Ben the reasons behind her and Tom's sham engagement, but there were limits to what she would open up about.

"I just don't," she said. Her voice was stiff, and she could feel her body stiffening, too. "Not everyone is obsessed with romantic relationships. And that's all I have to say on the subject."

He put a hand on her shoulder and squeezed. "Okay," he said. "I'll shut up now."

Ben had always seemed big and strong and powerful to her, while Jessica, in comparison, had often felt weak and trifling and insignificant. Sitting beside him now she felt the same contrast— him with his long, lean, loose-limbed body, relaxed and dynamic at the same time, and her sitting stiffly beside him in her crisp linen suit, prim and proper and negligible. Now even their body temperatures seemed to echo the differences between them, his hand warm and vital while she felt small and cold.

Heat seemed to seep into her through Ben's big, callused palm. She was intensely aware of his physicality—his hard-muscled strength, the warmth of his gaze, the dark stubble on his jaw.

She shifted away from him. "You didn't shave this morning."

He ran his hand over his chin. "No, I didn't. I showered, though. And I remembered my passport." He paused. "So, new topic. Do you want to talk about weather or sports or current events, or should we just go back to reading?"

"Well." Jessica glanced out the window. "The weather at thirty thousand feet is gorgeous. As for sports, the big event in Bermuda this week is their annual cricket match."

"Cricket?"

"Yes."

He sighed. "I had tickets to a Mets game this week."

She raised an eyebrow. "I didn't force you onto this plane, you know. In fact, I gave you a perfectly good out this morning."

"Yeah, I guess you did."

"So no complaints about missing the game."

"Agreed."

Jessica nodded toward the newspaper he'd stuck in the seat pocket. "So, anything interesting in the *Times*?"

CHAPTER FIVE

As the cabdriver drove briskly along the narrow, curving roads, Jessica felt a rush of pleasure. The breeze coming through the open window was warm and soft as it teased strands of hair across her face.

"Bermuda is beautiful," Ben said, looking out the other window at the lush vegetation and brightly painted houses.

"It is, isn't it? Even more beautiful than I imagined."

"You've never been here before?"

"No. My parents were never interested in coming, and I haven't traveled much on my own. Tom hasn't, either. That's one thing he and I were going to do together—travel. His job is so cutthroat that he never felt like he could take a vacation. He was going to take things a little easier after we were married, though."

It was odd to talk about those plans, as though she and Tom had been an ordinary couple planning a life together. And in a way, they had been. They would have been friends, companions, confidantes—everything but lovers.

A wave of melancholy went over her.

"It's okay to be sad about losing Tom, you know."

She turned her head to see Ben looking at her. Had he read her mind?

"But I didn't lose him. I mean, we weren't really together."

"Yeah, but you'd promised to share your life with him. And then you had the rug jerked out from under you."

Did she wish that Everett had never come into the picture? That she and Tom had gone through with their sham marriage?

No. Not just because it was the wrong thing for Tom, but because it was wrong for her, too. She didn't have a clear direction forward—not like Tom did—but she was glad they hadn't exchanged wedding vows.

"Thanks," she said to Ben. "But I'm okay. I mean . . . I wish it hadn't happened like that, but . . . I think it was the right thing. For both of us."

Her hand was on the seat between them, and Ben covered it with his. "Good," he said.

A dart of electricity went through her just as they took a curve a little too fast. She slid across the seat toward Ben, and for one dizzying moment she was almost in his lap, her hand still in his and their thighs pressed together. In the breathless seconds before she managed to scoot back to her side, her temperature seemed to go up twenty degrees.

"Sorry," she said, turning her head to look out the window again. Her face was red and her heart was pounding.

A minute later they turned onto a long drive, and a minute after that they pulled up in front of a sprawling, tangerine-colored hotel. A bellboy came out to meet them, collecting their luggage— well, her luggage, since Ben only had a carry-on—and telling them he'd bring it to their cottage.

"We have a cottage?" Ben asked Jessica as they entered the hotel, crossing the lobby toward the front desk.

She nodded. "Right on the beach."

"Wow. So are you going to tell the hotel people we're not actually—"

She stopped abruptly in the middle of the lobby.

"Absolutely not. I left New York to get away from all that, remember? I'm not going to share the details with a bunch of strangers."

"So if someone calls me Mr. Shelburne and congratulates me—"

"Just say thank you." She paused. "It probably won't come up, though. Tom and I chose this resort because it's not one of those all-inclusive places where the staff is in your face all the time. They'll give us our privacy."

"If you say so."

She glanced at the front desk. "The clerk will probably congratulate us if we check in together. If you want to avoid that, you could go on ahead and meet the bellboy at the cottage. It'll be the one closest to the ocean."

He grinned at her. "You're the boss, Jess. I'll see you in a few minutes."

She checked in at the desk, made a reservation for dinner at the hotel restaurant, and headed for the cottage herself.

The hotel's main building was on a rise above the ocean. A winding flagstone path led down to the water, passing the pool, poolside bar, and several small cottages before it reached the beach. Just before the path gave way to sand, it branched off to the right, heading toward the honeymoon cottage.

It was painted a bright cerulean blue and was surrounded by flowering bushes. The door stood open, and she could see Ben's broad back as he stood in the doorway, arms folded, surveying the interior.

"So what do you think?" she asked, coming up beside him. "We have our own path down to the ocean, and the concierge said . . ." She trailed off.

All right, this was awkward.

Really, really awkward.

Jessica had assumed from the phrase "honeymoon suite" that this place would be—well, a suite. With a separate living area and foldout couch, the way hotel suites were usually laid out.

There was a small sitting area but no couches. The place was basically one enormous bedroom, with one enormous bed.

A bed strewn with rose petals, of all ridiculous things.

It was a beautiful room. Big and bright and airy, with windows overlooking the ocean.

But all she could see was the bed.

The longer the two of them stood staring at that king-size behemoth, snow-white sheets and blankets providing the perfect backdrop for red rose petals, the more embarrassed she felt.

This was her fault. She should have confirmed the layout of the room, or something.

The truth was, she honestly hadn't thought about it. It hadn't mattered when it was going to be her and Tom, because—

"Where the hell was Tom going to sleep?" Ben asked.

She risked her first glance at him, and he was scowling. He looked so pissed off that she almost took a step back, but then she noticed the tips of his ears.

They were red. All through junior high, that had been a sure sign that he was embarrassed or uncomfortable about something.

That, oddly enough, made her feel a little better. At least she wasn't embarrassed all by herself.

"We were going to sleep in the same bed," she explained. "We've done it before. It's not an issue, because—"

"Because Tom's gay."

"Exactly."

He took a few steps into the room and stopped, glaring at the bed as though he blamed it for the current situation. "I'm not gay."

Didn't she know it.

He and Tom actually had similar builds. They were both tall, both rangy and powerful. Their faces were very different—Ben's was rough and craggy while Tom was more classically handsome—but in terms of what outside observers would characterize as "masculinity," the two men were very similar.

The difference was in her reaction to them.

For as long as she'd known him, Tom had inspired affection but not attraction. Because of that, he'd been her first kiss back in high school. She'd chosen him because he didn't make her feel uneasy or unsure of herself—not like Ben, for instance—and Tom had felt the same way about her. They weren't threatened by each other, and so experimenting with their first kiss had felt safe.

It hadn't been unpleasant, exactly, but no sparks had flown, either. They decided to "just be friends" after that, and a year later, Jessica was the first—and for a long time, the only—person he came out to.

When she saw Tom across a room, she felt a rush of warmth. He made her feel safe and secure and cared for. He would never ask anything of her she didn't know how to give, and because of that, he was one of the few people in the world Jessica allowed herself to be physically affectionate with.

Ben, on the other hand . . .

Her reaction to him had always been utterly different from her reaction to Tom. Sometime in eighth grade she'd tumbled onto the fact that she had a crush on him, and her feelings had been as intense as they were confusing.

Feverish excitement, anguished attraction. She couldn't describe the state she was in as pleasurable, and yet . . . whenever they were apart, she longed to be near him again.

Of course she'd hidden all that from him, allowing him to see only the outward signs of friendship. That was something else she and Tom had always shared: the ability to hide their true selves.

Even in high school, when she and Ben were no longer friends, her physical response to him had been the same. None of the boys she'd actually dated had come remotely close to making her feel that odd, unsettling combination of tingling excitement and overwhelming anxiety.

In a way, she'd been glad of that. There were a lot of reasons she didn't want to have anything to do with those kinds of feelings. She'd dated in high school and college because it was expected of her, and because not dating would have made her stand out. Given that, it probably wasn't a surprise that most of her relationships had been uninspiring, with more than one boyfriend breaking up with her because she didn't really seem "into" them.

That, she'd figured out eventually, was a euphemism for not enjoying sex enough.

Eventually she'd decided they were right. She didn't particularly enjoy sex. Her hormones didn't seem to function the way her friends' did, and there wasn't much she could do about it.

The one time she'd experienced typical teenage hormones was around Ben Taggart, and there had never been a possibility that she would act on her attraction to him.

But when she'd agreed to take this trip with him, why hadn't she realized that those feelings might still be there? Under the surface, ready to throw her off balance?

Because so much time had gone by. Because they hadn't seen each other in so long. And because she'd gotten used to her apparent immunity to physical attraction.

Last night had been full of warning signs she hadn't heeded. Warning signs that her female hormones might not be as dormant as she'd thought.

But she'd been able to hide her feelings when she was a teen. She was twenty-eight now, and a master at concealing things. All she had to do was act as though the problem of their sleeping arrangements was merely logistical.

She took a deep breath and let it out. "What do you suggest we do?"

"I suggest we call the front desk and switch rooms."

"They're all booked up. I told you that."

"Fine. Let's get a cot in here." He gestured toward the sitting area, which featured two armchairs and a small loveseat. "I'm six foot two, Jess. That's not going to cut it."

"We're in the honeymoon suite. We can't ask for a cot." She thought about it. "If I put the chairs together I could—"

"No way. You're sleeping in the bed. If you don't want to request a cot, I'll sleep on the floor."

"That's not a good solution," she objected.

He shrugged. "It's the best solution we've got. It won't be so bad."

"No." He'd come with her to Bermuda to support her, and she wasn't going to let him sleep on the floor. "I suppose there's no reason you and I can't do what Tom and I were going to do."

Ben stared at her in disbelief. "You mean share that bed?"

"Yes. Why not?"

"Do you need me to go over the part where I'm not gay?"

She rolled her eyes. "Come on, Ben. We're both adults. Are you telling me you'll be overcome by lust or something?"

"Of course I'm not saying that," he practically growled. "But it'll be . . ." He paused. "Awkward."

She shrugged. "Only if we let it be. I don't have a problem with it," she went on, glancing at the bed again.

A sudden image of the two of them in it together flashed through her mind, followed by a rush of heat.

"No problem at all," she repeated more firmly.

"Fine," Ben said after a moment. "Let's share a bed for ten days. That won't be weird at all. Why did I even think it might be?"

"It'll be fine. It's a really big bed," she pointed out.

He sighed. "Yeah, it is. But can we at least get rid of the rose petals?"

That made her smile.

"Definitely."

Ben glanced out the window. "How about we do that after going for a swim? I've never in my life seen water that gorgeous." He opened his carry-on and pulled out a pair of dark green bathing trunks. "Do you need the bathroom? If you don't, I'm going to change in there."

She shook her head. "I'll change out here."

Once the bathroom door closed behind him, she opened her suitcase and pulled out her own bathing suit. She changed quickly and called out, "I'll meet you down there, okay?"

"Okay," Ben called back.

She slipped on a pair of beach sandals, put a pair of sunglasses and a bottle of sunscreen into a tote bag, and went through the cottage's back door. It opened onto a patio and a private path down to the water.

She put the thought of sleeping arrangements out of her head. This trip was supposed to be an escape, and what better escape than swimming? She'd loved the ocean for as long as she could remember, and she had ten days of it to look forward to.

That's what she needed to focus on.

∾

It was a good thing he had a firm handle on his masculinity, because if he didn't, being told by a beautiful woman that sharing a bed with him wouldn't be the slightest bit awkward might have been a blow to his ego.

As it was, thanks to the firm-handle-on-his-masculinity thing, there was no problem at all.

Never mind that at his first glimpse of that king-size bed, all he'd been able to think about was him and Jessica in it together.

He'd pictured her lying naked on those silk sheets with him above her, ready to bury himself inside her. Not since he was a teenager had he been so overwhelmed by the visceral power of a sexual fantasy.

At least until Jessica had made it clear that he was the only one with that problem.

There was nothing like a woman's total lack of interest to calm a guy's libido. With Jessica completely unaffected by the thought of their sleeping together—sleeping next to each other, anyway—he should have no trouble tamping down his own feelings.

No trouble at all.

Then he went down to the ocean and saw Jessica in her bathing suit.

There were dozens of vacationers on the beach. Among the women, the preferred suit choice was a bikini. Bikinis with straps, bikinis without straps, bikinis of all colors, styles, and varieties. And given Jessica's predilection to be fashionable as well as to showcase her beauty, her suit should have been an unerring combination of classy and sexy.

But she was wearing a Speedo. A racing Speedo with thick cross straps—the kind worn by serious swimmers.

There was nothing enticing in the design of that suit. It conformed to Jessica's slender body, but not with any intention to be provocative.

He was surrounded by women in skimpy bikinis, and there, standing at the water's edge, stood a woman in a plain black one-piece.

And she was the woman he couldn't take his eyes off.

He'd accused her of being too skinny in high school. She was still too skinny as far as he was concerned, even though he knew society would consider her proportions perfect.

She was too skinny, she was wearing a boring-ass bathing suit, and she'd informed him a few minutes ago that sharing a bed with him would be just like sharing a bed with her gay friend.

And he was staring at her like a starving man at the first meal he'd seen in weeks.

Her skin was the most touchable he'd ever seen—smooth and creamy and begging to be kissed. And even though he thought she should put on a few pounds, Jessica's slim curves were undeniably appealing—including an ass so luscious it made his palms itch.

She was standing with her back to him, her hands on her hips, gazing out at the wide expanse of ocean. The beach was crowded and there were kids playing in the sand nearby, but she only had eyes for the vista before her.

He came up beside her. "Hey," he said.

She turned her head, surprised. "I didn't see you."

"I know. What were you thinking, just then?"

She looked back at the water. "Just that it's beautiful."

He stood there with her for a few minutes, drawn in by her fascination to be still and observant himself.

The sound of the ocean waves filled the air. The horizon seemed endless; the colors were deep and beautiful. The briny tang of the sea was all around them.

He nudged her elbow with his. "Happy you came?"

She kept her eyes on the ocean, but she was smiling. "Yes."

A memory of the last time the two of them had been swimming flashed before his mind's eye. "Do you remember the pool at Shipley?" he asked.

Unexpectedly, her smile dimmed. "Don't remind me."

61

Her response confused him. "But you loved that pool. You went swimming every chance you got."

"Yes, I did. Looking like a whale."

"Hey!"

She looked at him, startled. "What is it?"

He held her eyes with his. "I hereby establish the first ground rule for this trip. You're not allowed to body-shame yourself like that, even if it's your past self. You were beautiful in eighth grade, Jess. You've always been beautiful."

He could see her resistance to that notion in the ripple of tension that passed over her face, but he kept his gaze locked with hers.

Finally she shrugged. "Fine. But if you get to establish a ground rule, then so do I."

"Fair enough. What is it?"

She blinked. "Well, I haven't thought of it yet. But I will. And when I do, you have to obey it blindly."

That made him smile. "Okay," he said. "I will."

She looked back at the water again. "I'm going in."

She walked out into the waves, striding forward until she was waist deep. Then she dove in gracefully, swimming underwater long enough that Ben started to feel anxious. He breathed a sigh of relief when she popped up much farther out, swimming strongly.

He was so focused on watching her that he forgot he'd intended to swim himself. But before he could rectify that, he felt a hand tugging on his.

"Hey, mister? Will you play with us?"

"Huh?"

He blinked down at the kid who'd accosted him. He was about nine or ten years old, and he wasn't alone. Another munchkin, maybe a year or two younger, was standing next to him.

"We want to play Frisbee in the water, but Gram says we can't until our dad gets back. So will you play with us?"

The grandmother in question was relaxing on one of the lounge chairs higher up on the beach. Ben glanced out to where Jessica was doing an impeccable crawl and then back down at the little boy looking up at him so hopefully.

"Let's go check with your Gram," he said resignedly.

The elderly woman smiled when he introduced himself. "Have at it," she said, waving her hand toward the water. "Just don't go in too deep," she added to her grandchildren.

They started a game of Frisbee with elaborate scoring rules he never quite understood. The kids, of course, were tireless, and so distracting that he didn't notice that Jessica had swum up next to him until he heard her voice.

"Wow, that was fast," she said, sounding amused.

"Hey," he said, swiveling his head and consequently missing the Frisbee that had just been thrown at him.

He fished it out of the water and tossed it to one of the kids. Their father had joined them a few minutes before, so he took the opportunity to excuse himself from the game.

He kept his eyes on Jessica as they headed toward the shore. She looked like a mermaid with her fine blonde hair dripping down her back and droplets of water clinging to her pale shoulders.

"What was fast?" he asked her.

She gestured toward the boys he'd been playing with. "You're such a kid magnet. It never fails. Give it five minutes, and every kid in the vicinity will be hanging off you." She grinned at him. "Maybe they sense you're a softy."

He hadn't seen her smile like that in years—like she didn't have a care in the world.

"You think I'm a softy, huh?"

She ran her hands over her wet hair, twisting it into a long rope and wringing the water out. "Are you kidding? You've been a sucker for kids your whole life—not to mention stray animals and lost causes. You have a savior complex."

They crossed the sand toward the lounge chair where she'd left her bag.

"I like kids, sure—that's why I became a teacher. But you're the one who's a sucker for animals, and I don't have a savior complex. And where are you getting the lost-cause thing?"

"Well, what do you call me?"

He stopped walking. When she realized it, she stopped, too, and turned to look at him.

"I don't think you're a lost cause," he said. "I've never thought that."

She looked skeptical. "Really?"

"Yeah. Really."

"You thought I was so pathetic that you put your life on hold to come with me on this trip. You think I need saving, Ben."

"Even if I did, that wouldn't make you a lost cause."

"Okay, then. What makes you think I'm *not* a lost cause?"

He ran a finger along one of her Speedo straps. "This."

She stared at him. "What?"

"This bathing suit. It's old and a little bit frayed here and there. It's not fashionable. The only reason for you to wear it is because it makes you happy. *Swimming* makes you happy. And as long as there's one thing in this world you do because it brings you joy, then you're not a lost cause."

Her gaze fell. She looked down at her toes curling in the sand, and didn't say anything for a minute.

"You're right," she said finally.

"About what?"

"Swimming. I do love it. As long as I can remember, it's been the one thing I do just because I enjoy it."

"Okay, then. There's your blueprint."

She looked up again. "My blueprint? My blueprint for what?"

"For the rest of your life. Your life post wedding."

"Post getting jilted at the altar, you mean?"

He grinned at her. "Exactly."

She folded her arms. "All right, then. Tell me about this blueprint."

"You carved out a tiny space for yourself with swimming. Something that's an honest reflection of who you are, something you actually enjoy doing for its own sake. Now all you have to do is make that space a little bigger. For the rest of this trip, focus on doing things just because you want to do them."

"And how will that help me?"

"On the plane you said you don't know who you are. You need to figure that out. This will help."

She froze for a second, and then she turned away and finished the walk to her lounge chair. She'd left a beach towel there, and now she draped it over her shoulders.

"I pissed you off," he said, coming up behind her. "I'm sorry."

She kept her back to him. "You didn't piss me off. It's just . . . I don't need you to fix me. Okay?"

He walked around to the other side of the chair so he could look her in the eyes. "Okay," he said.

A few seconds ticked by. Then:

"I'm going to go back to the cottage," she said. "Would you mind staying out here for a bit? I'd love some privacy. If you give me an hour, I'll return the favor."

"Sure, I'll stay out here for a while." He smiled. "I hear they have a hot tub next to the bar. I'll be fine."

"All right. Thanks, Ben."

As he watched her pack up her tote bag and go over to the spigot where you could wash the sand from your feet, he wondered what had just happened.

There had been a genuine moment of connection.

Jessica had seemed physically softer, as though the tension she always carried with her had lifted briefly. As though he'd found a way past her defenses.

Then he'd pushed her too far.

Maybe Jessica was right. Maybe he did have a savior complex.

He shook his head slowly. He should do what he'd told her to do: focus on having a good time for the next ten days.

It was time to visit the open-air bar and order the Bermuda rum swizzle he'd heard so much about.

CHAPTER SIX

I t felt luxurious to have the room to herself.

If she'd been braver, she could have come to Bermuda alone—and this beautiful suite would have been all hers. No awkwardness about sleeping arrangements . . . and nothing else she didn't want to deal with, either.

You said you don't know who you are. You need to figure that out.

But did she want to figure it out?

She'd never wanted to before. Because at the very core of herself, there were things she didn't want to face.

Maybe that was why she'd let Ben come with her. Because when you don't know yourself—or when you're afraid to know yourself—the last thing you want is to be alone. That was one of the reasons she and Tom had decided to get married, after all. Because neither one of them wanted to be alone.

Being alone meant looking inside. And that, to her, was far more dangerous than spending ten days on an island with Ben Taggart.

Or so she'd thought.

You said you don't know who you are. You need to figure that out.

No, she didn't. What she needed to do was figure out a way to get through the days . . . to get through her life . . . now that her partner in cowardice had deserted her.

And she needed to get back to her mission statement for this trip: getting away from hard questions and painful memories and having a good time.

A few hours later, waiting for Ben in the hotel lounge, she decided that alcohol would help with that mission. She downed two martinis in quick succession, and waited for the warm flush of relaxation to follow.

But before the vodka had a chance to fully kick in, Ben joined her at the bar.

He was dressed, she was glad to see, in a charcoal-gray suit and maroon tie. He'd shaved, too.

After they were shown to their table—a spot next to a window with a view of the ocean—she said, "You're wearing a suit for the second time in two days."

He smiled. "Yeah. And both times because of you."

"I'm amazed you even brought a suit—and that it came out of your carry-on looking so good."

"I didn't bring a suit. I bought this at the hotel boutique."

"You did?"

He nodded. "I knew there was a dress code at this restaurant, and I didn't want to embarrass you."

That was surprisingly sweet. "Well, you look very nice."

As she heard the words come out of her mouth, she winced a little. She sounded so . . . prim.

"You look nice, too."

"Thanks." She had put her accustomed armor back in place, in the form of a pink silk A-line Prada dress, a pair of Manolo Blahnik flats, and perfect hair and makeup. The French manicure she'd gotten for the wedding was still flawless, so her nails were perfect, too. She looked down at her hands now, her fingers tipped with those impeccable white crescents.

"You know what?" Ben said. "I take it back."

His voice was different. Rougher. Startled, she looked up to meet his eyes.

"You don't look nice, Jess. You look incredible. Beautiful. Stunning, even."

Her heart beat faster. Was that the reason for the sudden warmth heating her cheeks, or were her two martinis finally kicking in?

She didn't know what to say. Before she could say anything, their waiter came to the table and took their dinner order. After he was gone, Ben leaned forward again.

"In case you're worried, I'm not coming on to you. I'm just being honest." He paused for a moment. "After you shut me down this afternoon, I figured I wouldn't push you. But when I thought more about it, I realized something. I realized that I might be the only person in your life willing to be honest with you right now— and who you can be honest with."

A spasm of anxiety tightened her belly, and she tried to lighten the mood. "Come on, Ben—we haven't even had appetizers yet. It's too early in the evening to be this intense."

He smiled a little. "We don't have to be intense—just honest. And if that's not something you want, okay. If you don't like my proposal, I'll get on a plane and out of your hair."

She reached for a roll, trying to conceal how much she didn't like that idea. "You have a proposal, huh? What is it?"

"That you think of this trip as a safe space. What happens in Bermuda stays in Bermuda."

"That's what you said on the plane. That I could say anything to you and it wouldn't matter. That I could tell the truth without repercussions."

"Exactly. If you're willing to do that . . . to tell me what you really think about things, to try to be honest for the next ten days . . . then I'll stay. But I'm not up for a week of small talk and polite lies."

She felt frustration rising. "So all I have to do is tell you what I really think. But what if I don't want to talk about whatever it is you want to talk about? What if *that's* what I really think? You're making it sound like if I don't say what you want to hear, you're just going to pack up and leave. That's not fair."

He shook his head. "That's not what I'm saying. I just want our conversations to be real."

"What does that mean? Give me an example."

"Why did you stop being friends with me after eighth grade?"

She stared at him. "So being real means digging up the past?"

"Among other things, yeah. But I've wanted to ask you that question for fifteen years, and it seems like this is my chance."

As she locked eyes with Ben, she flashed back to their younger selves. Her: overweight and insecure and damaged in ways Ben didn't know anything about. Him: good-looking and athletic and rebellious . . . and one of her best friends.

Until he wasn't.

Did she want to talk about this? Could she talk about this?

She didn't have to. She could get up and leave right now. She could go back to the suite and order room service, and Ben, as true to his word as she was sure he would be, would pack up his things and head back to New York.

She took a deep breath. "There were a lot of reasons."

"Give me one."

She looked down at the roll she'd buttered so carefully. "I'd lost all that weight, and I was starting high school. I was tired of being a loser, and I wanted things to be different. I wanted to be popular. I know that never mattered to you, but it mattered to me. And it seemed like the best way to get there was to turn my back on the past."

She couldn't tell him everything she'd turned her back on. She could never tell him the whole truth. But this was part of the truth, and she hoped it would be enough.

It was all so long ago. It seemed silly that they were even talking about this, and yet . . .

Ben had wanted to ask her this question for fifteen years. When she thought about that, she realized there was something she'd wanted to say to him for fifteen years, too.

"I'm sorry," she said suddenly.

"Sorry for what?" Ben asked, sounding genuinely surprised.

Somehow, that made her feel a little bit braver. Ben didn't expect anything from her; he wasn't demanding anything of her. He'd just wanted to know what had happened between them so long ago. He'd lost a friend back in junior high, and he'd never understood why.

She couldn't tell him all the reasons why. But she could at least apologize.

"I'm sorry I pushed you away back then. I'm sorry we stopped being friends."

The waiter arrived with their first course, and for a moment they focused on eating. Then:

"I'm sorry, too," Ben said.

She finished a bite of her salad. "Sorry for what?"

"Sorry I didn't fight for our friendship. I could have tried to talk to you about it, but I was too proud."

"I don't blame you for that," she said, surprised that he would blame himself. "And anyway," she added wryly, "I wouldn't have listened to you. I'd made my decision, and nothing would have changed my mind."

Ben looked thoughtful. "You changed so much that year. It was like you wanted to be a different person."

She *had* wanted to be a different person. She'd done everything she could to bury her old life and reinvent herself as someone new.

Someone untouchable. Invulnerable. Safe.

And if that had meant severing ties with the person who'd been her friend through thick and thin—the boy who'd had her back when the other kids taunted her—well, that had been a price she was willing to pay.

But the same dark secret that made her willing to pay that price was the same secret she couldn't share—not then and not now. Because of that, she could never be completely honest with Ben.

But she could give him as much truth as she was capable of.

"I hated myself when I was fat. When my parents sent me to that camp and I finally lost the weight, all I wanted to do was forget the person I'd been. And once I started it was hard to stop."

"Started?"

"With the new crowd. With the whole popularity thing. It kind of sucks you in, I guess."

"Like the Mafia?"

She smiled down at her salad. "Sort of."

"I hated the people you hung out with in high school."

She looked up again, raising one eyebrow. "Really? I never would have guessed."

"Yeah, I know I wasn't subtle. But you made some good friends in college. Your roommates, what were their names? Kate and Sharon?"

"Kate and Simone."

"Right. I met them a few times, when you brought them to your parents' parties."

"Back in the day when Amelia could still drag you to those?"

He smiled. "Yeah. Anyway, they seemed nice."

"They were. They are."

Jessica felt a familiar pang. She'd always felt at a disadvantage with her two college roommates. On some level, she believed they were too good for her—although not in the way that her mother and her friends thought of themselves as "too good" for people.

Kate and Simone were good in a deeper sense: principled, generous, honest, brave.

Kind of like Ben.

A wave of depression went through her. She could feel the weight of all the good people she didn't deserve—Kate, Simone, Ben, Tom. People who knew who they were or who had the courage to try and find out.

"What's wrong?" Ben asked.

"What do you mean?"

"You looked sad just then. What were you thinking about?"

Ben's eyes were warm as he looked at her. Interested.

This was the way he'd looked at her on the plane, and at the wedding reception. He wasn't asking questions just to make conversation.

He really wanted to know the answers.

And he'd promised her that what was said in Bermuda would stay in Bermuda. So why not talk about what she was thinking? What she was feeling?

Maybe it was the alcohol in her system, but she was starting to think it might not be such a terrible idea after all.

"You know what you said before? That I need to figure out who I am?"

He nodded.

She took a deep breath. "I'm afraid there is no me."

Ben stopped with his fork halfway to his mouth. Then he set the fork back down on his plate. "What are you talking about?"

"If you spend enough time being someone you're not, you lose who you are." She groped for words to explain. "I'm afraid that if I go looking for who I am, there won't be anything there to find."

She'd half expected Ben to be horrified at her admission. Of all the people she'd known in her life, he was the least likely to lose touch with who he was.

But he didn't look horrified.

One of her hands was clenched in her lap; the other was on the table. Ben reached out and covered that hand with his.

"So figure it out now."

She thought about pulling her hand away, but the truth was, another person's touch was comforting.

No—not just another person's touch.

Ben's touch.

But that didn't change the fact that she couldn't do what he wanted her to do.

"It's too late," she said.

"I don't believe that. I'm not a big believer in fate, but maybe that's why we ended up on this trip together."

She frowned. "What do you mean?"

"I knew you when you were a kid. When you did things because you wanted to." He paused. "When you had that Backstreet Boys poster, for example."

That made her smile. "I don't like the Backstreet Boys anymore. Remember?"

"Thank God. But remembering what you used to like is just a start. We'll also figure out what you enjoy now."

"We will? How?"

"We'll experiment."

The grin he gave her was probably perfectly innocent, but Jessica felt a quick rush of electricity. The words *we'll experiment*, spoken in Ben's smooth baritone voice, took on a double meaning.

But that was only in her head. Ben had made it clear he wasn't coming on to her. He'd said so.

The waiter came by to clear their salads and deliver the main course, and once again their attention turned to food.

"How's your fish?" Ben asked after a moment, and she glanced up at him.

"I thought we weren't allowed to make small talk."

"I didn't mean we couldn't make *any* small talk. I just don't want our conversation to be *all* small talk."

"Ah. Well, in that case, my fish is wonderful. How's your steak?"

"Also wonderful."

"And how is—"

The sound of a ringtone interrupted her, and Ben frowned. "Sorry," he said, reaching into his breast pocket and pulling out his phone. "Let me—" He glanced at the screen and his expression changed. "Damn. Do you mind if I answer this? I won't be long."

"Of course. Go ahead."

He hit Accept. "Jamal? I'm so sorry." He listened for a minute. "Yeah, I know, but I have a really good excuse. I'm in Bermuda." The person on the other end spoke again, and Ben's eyes met hers for a moment. "A friend," he said. "I'll give you the whole story soon, okay? Good luck tonight, and I'm sorry I can't be there."

Jessica felt a rush of guilt as he slid the phone back into his pocket. "You're missing something. What is it?"

"A friend of mine is reading at a poetry slam."

She blinked. "A poetry slam? Really? I didn't think people actually did those."

He took a bite of steak. "Most people shouldn't. But Jamal is an English teacher and a great writer. He'll do a great job."

"I'm sorry you can't be there. Are you missing anything else because of me?"

Ben finished his bite before he spoke. "Nothing important. But if I were, it would be my choice. It was my idea to come with you on this trip." He smiled at her. "And I'm really glad I did."

That was nice.

She smiled back at him. "So your friend is an English teacher, huh? At your school?"

"Yes."

"I heard that you won a Teacher of the Year award a couple of years ago. Was it at that school? How long have you taught there?"

"Five years."

"And you teach math?"

"Math and computer science." He hesitated. "Actually, I'm taking a new job this fall."

"You are? At a different school?"

"Yeah." He hesitated again. "It's in Chicago, actually."

She stared at him. "Chicago? You mean . . . you're leaving New York?"

"That's the plan."

Ben wasn't part of her life and hadn't been for a long time. So why did she feel so dismayed at this news?

"Well," she said after a moment. "A lot of people will miss you. What's in Chicago?"

"An experiment. Someone I met in college is starting an inner-city program for at-risk kids that could be a template for urban school districts around the country. She offered me a chance to be a part of it, and I said yes."

"Oh." She paused. "That sounds exciting. But won't you miss your friends and family?"

He nodded. "Yeah, of course. But sometimes it's good to start something new." He took his last bite of steak and sat back in his chair. "That's what you have a chance to do, Jess. Start a new chapter in your life."

The waiter came to clear their dishes and offer dessert menus. Ben took one but Jessica shook her head, and he looked at her quizzically.

"Are you sure you don't want to look? You're on vacation, after all."

"I know, but I don't eat dessert."

"Sure you do. Or you did, anyway. Why did you stop?"

She frowned. "Come on, Ben. You know why."

"Because of your weight?"

She shrugged. "It's not just about appearance," she said. "It's also about health. I wasn't at a healthy weight in junior high. I don't want to go back to that." She paused. "Anyway, I've been on a diet for fifteen years. I'm used to it."

Ben was quiet for a moment, glancing over the menu before meeting her eyes again. "How about this. I'll order dessert, and you can have a bite if you want one."

That sounded doable—and tempting. "What dessert would you pick?"

He grinned and held out the menu. "They all look good to me. What looks good to you?"

She took the menu from him and ran her eyes down the listings. Apple tart, flourless chocolate cake, bread pudding—

Hot fudge sundae.

"Okay, I can tell by the look in your eyes that you've found it. Which one?"

He could read her that easily?

She frowned at him over the top of the menu. "The hot fudge sundae, if you must know."

Ben looked delighted, which was kind of sweet. "You used to love ice cream, so that makes sense. Let's order it."

"But I'm only going to have one bite."

"One perfect, delectable bite." He called the waiter over and placed their order—a hot fudge sundae and two cocktails. Then he sat back and looked at her.

"What do you want to do after dinner?"

She sighed. "I was going to start on the notes to all the people who sent wedding gifts so I have them ready when I get back to New York. I brought the stationery with me."

"No way."

She blinked. "I'm sorry?"

"I'm not kidding. I'll burn that stationery if I have to, but I'm not letting you do anything wedding-related on this trip. I didn't ask what you *should* do after dinner. I asked what you *want* to do. If you were here to have fun, what would you do?"

She looked out the window at the dark night. Clouds had rolled in since that afternoon, covering the moon and stars, but she could see lanterns twinkling along the path that led down to the ocean.

"Take a walk on the beach, I guess."

"Okay, then. That's what we'll do."

"But all those gifts—"

"Can wait. What's going to happen if you wait ten days to write those notes?"

She thought about it. "Nothing, I guess. But I hate thinking of it hanging over me."

"So don't think about it. Forget about it until you get back. Better yet, when you get back, ask your sister to deal with it. She's your maid of honor."

"I couldn't do that."

"Sure you could. But you can figure that out when you're home. For now, you're on vacation in Bermuda with a hot fudge sundae and a dark and stormy on the way."

"That reminds me. What's a dark and stormy, and why did you order me one?"

"It's rum and ginger beer, and I ordered it for you because that's one of the drinks Bermuda is famous for." He looked up as the waiter arrived, setting their cocktails in front of them. "If you don't like it, I'll drink it."

She lifted the heavy crystal glass and took a hesitant sip.

"Okay, it's good."

"Perfect," Ben said as the waiter set down their ice cream. "And since we already know you like hot fudge sundaes, I think our project is off to a pretty good start."

"Project? What project?"

"The Finding Out What Jessica Likes and Getting Her to Do Those Things project."

"That's a really long title," she said, looking at the enormous sundae on the table between them. She dug her spoon into the ice cream, making sure to get a good dollop of fudge and whipped cream.

She put the bite in her mouth and gave a moan of pleasure. "Oh my God, that's good."

Ben didn't say anything, and she glanced up. He was staring at her with an odd expression.

"What is it?"

He shook his head and picked up his own spoon.

"Nothing's wrong. I like to see you enjoying yourself, that's all." He took a bite, and then it was his turn to make a sound of pleasure.

"You're enjoying it too, huh?"

"Yeah." He lifted his dark and stormy, smiling at her over the rim. "But I enjoy things all the time. It's more of a special occasion for you."

Ben did enjoy things. He always had.

A sudden memory of their senior year of high school flashed before her mind's eye.

Ben had dated Alexis Shaw for most of that year. They didn't do a lot of PDAs, or maybe Jessica just didn't see them. But one day she'd caught sight of them in an empty classroom. They were leaning up against a wall, kissing. That's all it had been—just kissing. But something in the way they'd abandoned themselves so completely to each other had twisted her insides.

She would never be that free with someone. That lustful. That happy.

"Would you like another bite?"

She came back to the present when Ben asked that question, gesturing with his spoon toward the sundae.

She found herself thinking of him in the ocean that afternoon, his bare torso hard and sculpted and golden in the sun. Then she flashed back to the teenage boy he'd been, kissing his girlfriend like it was the most important thing he'd ever do.

Her cheeks burned. What had made her think of that long-ago moment? And why was she picturing him in his bathing suit?

"No, thanks," she said, lowering her eyes and taking another sip of her drink.

The meal drew to an end soon after. When Jessica rose from her chair, a wave of dizziness made her realize that two martinis and a very strong dark and stormy had, in fact, made themselves felt.

Aha! That's why she was thinking of Ben in his bathing suit. She was tipsy.

Ben offered her his arm as they left the restaurant, and she started to giggle.

He raised an eyebrow. "What's so funny?"

"You being formal."

He smiled down at her. "I wasn't being formal. I was just trying to keep you from falling down. You seem a little, uh, exhilarated."

"Exhilarated? That's the best euphemism for being drunk I've ever heard." She threw her hands up in the air. "I'm exhilarated!"

Ben took one of her hands and tucked it under his arm. "Good for you. Now let's go take that walk by the beach."

But when they reached the doors at the other end of the lobby, they saw through the glass that it had begun to rain.

"Wait here," Ben told her. "I'll grab an umbrella from the front desk."

Jessica nodded. But after he left, some impulse made her push through the doors to the shelter of the portico.

Outside she could hear the rain as well as see it. It pattered down onto the roof above her, the grassy lawn, and the flagstones of the path that led to the ocean.

As a kid, she'd loved summer showers. She'd loved jumping from puddle to puddle in Central Park, her skin warm and wet and her hair heavy with rainwater. She remembered smoothing it back from her face until it was as sleek as a seal's pelt.

Of course it was against her mother's rules to go out in the rain without an umbrella. But that had been in the days when she would still, once in a while, do something she wasn't supposed to do.

Before she realized what she intended, she'd stepped out from under the portico roof and onto the flagstone path.

The rain was coming down harder now, and it didn't take long for her to get soaking wet.

"Jess!"

That was Ben, coming to her rescue.

She turned just as he reached her, opening the umbrella he'd brought to shelter her from the rain.

"What happened? Why'd you come out here?"

This was quintessential Ben—concerned for others, not noticing or caring about his own comfort. He was holding the umbrella over her and getting wet himself, but it was obvious he wasn't worried about that.

"You're soaked," he said, frowning down at her.

He was so handsome and strong. So kind, so warmhearted, so comfortable in his own skin.

Everything she wasn't. Everything she could never be.

Years ago, when they were friends, Ben had tried to put some of his warmth and bravery into her. He'd failed, but that hadn't stopped him from trying again—right up until the moment she'd pushed him away for good.

And now, years later, he'd shown up in her life at her very worst moment, trying to help her stand on her feet again.

Trying to give her shelter from the rain.

She took the umbrella from him and tossed it aside.

"What the—"

She put her hands on his shoulders. The material of his suit was wet beneath her palms, and she moved her hands to his face.

He went absolutely still when she did that, staring down at her.

"What are you doing, Jess?"

His voice was gruff, wary . . . but there was something else there, too.

Desire.

"I want something."

The rain was coming down harder. Another couple came out of one of the cottages and hurried toward them, staring in astonishment before scurrying into the shelter of the hotel lobby.

She could feel Ben's jaw tighten under her hands. "Wanting something doesn't always make it a good idea."

She shook her head slowly. "Oh, no. You don't get to say that to me now, after you spent the last twenty-four hours telling me I should do what I want."

His dark eyes seemed to glitter in the light that spilled out of the hotel windows. His chest was rising and falling with more effort than she would have thought necessary for someone just standing still.

"Jessica—"

"You hardly ever call me that."

"Call you what?"

"Jessica."

She saw his Adam's apple jump as he swallowed. "Jess, then."

"No."

"No, what?"

"I liked it. Call me Jessica again."

He closed his eyes briefly and opened them again. Then he took hold of her wrists and moved her hands away from his face.

"Jessica," he said, and the low rumble of his voice saying the three syllables of her name made her shiver. "I don't think—"

"Ben. Ben. What about the project? Finding Out What Jessica Likes?"

"I just—"

"What are you protecting me from now?"

"What do you mean?"

"You don't even know what I'm going to ask you, and you're already protecting me from whatever it is. What do you think I'm going to ask?"

He took a deep breath. "You're right. I don't know. What is it you want to do?"

"I want to go swimming."

His eyebrows rose. "That's it?"

She was tempted to cross her fingers behind her back, but he still held her wrists. "That's it." Suddenly enjoying herself immensely, she smiled up at him. "Why, Ben, what did you think I was going to say?"

He released her hands. "You want to go swimming in the rain?"

"Yes. I've always wanted to, but it's not the kind of thing people do. According to you, though, I can do whatever I want on this trip. Of course, that doesn't mean you have to go with me. I don't mind going alone."

"Are you kidding? I'm not letting you swim alone at night. I'm coming with you."

Excellent.

"Okay, then."

The lobby doors opened and an older couple came out, exclaiming in dismay at the rain beyond the shelter of the porch. When they saw Ben and Jessica standing in the downpour, they stared in bewilderment.

"Here," Ben said, stooping to grab their discarded umbrella and walking over to hand it to them. "Apparently we won't be needing this."

When he came back to Jessica, he crooked his elbow with all the aplomb of an escort at a grand ball. "Shall we?" he asked.

She laid her hand primly on his arm. "Yes, indeed."

Then they walked sedately down the flagstone path.

There was something beautifully surreal about strolling through the pouring rain in their evening clothes. Most people were safely in their rooms or in the restaurant, but every so often someone would go scurrying past, holding an umbrella or a jacket over their heads. And she and Ben walked along as though there weren't a cloud in the sky.

They were soaked to the skin. After a minute Ben said, "Your dress is probably ruined. Not to mention your shoes."

"I know."

"You don't mind?"

"Nope."

His arm under her hand felt strong and warm and solid, even encased in a rain-soaked suit jacket. Everything about him was strong and warm and solid.

He started to turn when the path branched off toward their cottage, but Jessica tugged on his arm. "The beach is this way."

"Sure, but aren't we going to change?"

She laughed and dropped his arm, spinning around in a circle. "What for? We might as well go in like this." She kicked off her shoes and reached down to pick them up. "I'll race you to the water," she called over her shoulder, starting to run barefoot toward the beach.

He caught up with her almost immediately, of course, and by the time she felt the sand under her feet, he was already at the water's edge.

He turned and faced her as she came to a stop, laughing.

"My God," she gasped. "I haven't run like that in years."

He grinned down at her. "It suits you," he said.

"It does?"

"Your face is glowing."

She pressed her palms to her face. "How can you tell?"

The nearest light came from the windows of the cottages and the lanterns along the path, and there couldn't be enough to see the color of her cheeks.

"I can tell," was all he said. Then he kicked off his own shoes, peeled off his socks, removed his jacket and tie, and tossed them onto the sand. "I hope my phone stays dry."

"How much are you planning to take off?" she asked.

"This is it," he said, wading into the water in his pants and dress shirt. "What about you?"

"I'm good," she said, wading out beside him.

The falling rain made music on the water. At night, the ocean seemed even bigger: dark and mysterious and unknown.

Her dress floated up in a circle around her.

"You look like some kind of water fairy," Ben said. "The spirit of a water lily, or something."

He was waist deep and she was up to her shoulders. Between the ocean and the rain, she was surrounded by water but still able to breathe, as though she really were some kind of sea spirit—a mermaid or other creature that could live underwater.

She closed her eyes for a moment, her face upturned. After a moment Ben asked, "Do you want to swim?"

She opened her eyes and turned to face him. After parading through the rain in a new Prada, she should have felt capable of anything—but she was suddenly so nervous her heart raced.

"I want something else," she said.

And before he could answer or back away, she slid her arms around his neck and pulled him down for a kiss.

CHAPTER SEVEN

From the moment he'd seen Jessica with her pink silk dress plastered to her body, Ben had been struggling to overcome his baser instincts. She was tipsy, for one thing—and she'd been left at the altar the day before. She was the poster child of a vulnerable woman no man had the right to take advantage of.

He'd redoubled his efforts when she'd put her hands on his face, even though she'd looked so beautiful in that moment she'd taken his breath away.

Once they were in the ocean he'd relaxed his guard a bit, figuring this rain-soaked night swim was her way to let off some steam . . . steam that might otherwise have led to a one-night stand she'd regret the moment it was over.

Maybe that was why she managed to take him by surprise. Whatever the reason, when she kissed him, his mind short-circuited and his instincts took over.

She smelled like the ocean and tasted like rainwater, and the instant their lips touched, his arms went around her.

His heart slammed against his ribs as he pulled her close. She made a noise in her throat, and for a second he was afraid he'd hurt her.

Then she gripped his shoulders and pressed herself against him. Electricity surged through him as his tongue slid into her mouth. She was hot silk and sweet fire and rain-warmed skin, and her hunger and need were so unexpected that for a few feverish moments he forgot everything but kissing her—kissing her with so much intensity that the fusion of their mouths felt like alchemy.

But when she reached through the water for the waistband of his pants, he dragged his mouth from hers.

"No," he panted, his body throbbing with so much heat he half expected the pelting rain to steam when it hit his skin.

Jessica's blue eyes looked huge and dark as she stared up at him. She was panting, too, and her lips were so damn tempting he had to look away for a moment.

"Why can't we?" she asked, grabbing the front of his shirt as he tried to take a step back. "You said I should do things just because I want to. You said I should experiment. You said—"

The tremble in her voice and the feel of her small hands fisted in his shirt were doing things to him he didn't want to think about. "I didn't mean you should experiment with *me*," he said roughly, trying to control himself.

"But—"

"Stop."

She stared at him. "Are you angry?"

"What? No! Of course not."

"But your voice is all growly."

"That's because I'm trying really, really hard not to rip your clothes off right now."

"But that's what I want you to do!"

"No, you don't."

She let go of his shirt with one hand, but only so she could smack him on the arm. "Don't you dare tell me what I want after you harangued me about finding myself."

He held up his hands in a gesture of surrender. "Okay, you're right. I'm sorry. I didn't mean to do that. I just . . ." He bowed his head and let the rain fall on the back of his neck. "Look, I don't claim to be a saint, but . . . there's no way I could live with myself if something happened between us tonight. You've been drinking, and—"

"Only that dark and stormy—and, well, the martinis I had before dinner."

"You had martinis before dinner?"

"Two."

"I didn't know that. Okay, so you've *really* been drinking. Not to mention you've had a pretty traumatic twenty-four hours. Even if you signed a contract in your own blood swearing I wasn't taking advantage of you, I'd never be able to absolve myself."

"But—"

He closed his hands over hers. "Listen to me. If you still feel this way tomorrow morning, it'll be a different story."

She blinked. "You mean . . . if I still want you in the morning . . . then we can sleep together?"

His heart clenched in his chest—and other parts of his anatomy tightened as well. "Yeah," he said gently. "If you feel the same in the harsh light of day, I'll be with you in a heartbeat. Okay?"

"Well . . . okay."

Her head dipped down, and she heaved a sigh. "So . . . I guess we should go back to the room, huh?"

She looked so depressed that his heart twisted again.

"Are you kidding? It's incredible out here. I'm not ready to go back yet."

She looked up. "Are you sure?"

"Hell yes. No deeper than this, though, okay? It's dark and I don't want to lose you in a tragic drowning accident."

"Okay," Jessica said.

She took a step away from him. Then she tipped herself backward and floated supine, closing her eyes and lifting her face to the rain.

He stayed by her side, holding her hand but letting her drift. As the minutes went by, the rain lessened and then stopped altogether. Once it did, he became more aware of the sounds of the ocean—the lapping of the waves against the dock and the beach.

After a while he stretched out on the water and floated beside Jessica, gazing up at the cloud-covered sky.

The wind freshened, and a ghostly crescent moon gleamed through a rent in the clouds. When they parted farther, a sprinkling of stars glowed against the velvety sky.

"It's so beautiful," Jessica said beside him, her voice low and rich and clear.

"Yeah," he agreed. "It is."

They floated for another minute of blissful silence. And then, suddenly, there was saltwater in his face and Jessica was laughing.

"What the—"

He stood upright again as he realized that Jessica had splashed him. "I can't believe you did that," he said.

"Well, I wanted to do it. And I have it on good authority that if I do things just because I want to do them—"

He didn't let her finish. He grabbed her around the waist and tossed her, grinning when she came up sputtering a few yards away.

"I can't believe you did that," she gasped.

"Believe it, lady."

She flung her wet hair back and grinned at him. "Are you ready to go in?"

"I guess so."

They thrashed their way to shore, and Ben grabbed their things. Then they walked barefoot up the beach to the path and from there to the cottage.

"You should take the bathroom first," Ben said at the door. "I'll wait out here."

"You don't want to come inside?"

"I'll just drip all over everything," he said. "I'd rather stay on the patio and stargaze."

"You'll get cold," she objected.

"No, it's a warm night. I'll be fine."

"Well . . . all right. I'll be quick."

"Take your time, Jess. I'm fine out here."

The truth was, he wanted a chance to recover his composure a little bit. Seeing Jessica come out of the water like a mermaid, her dress clinging to her like a second skin, he'd gotten so hard so fast he was glad for the darkness and a bundle of clothes he could hold in front of himself.

Once Jessica was safely behind the closed door, Ben sank down onto one of the patio chairs and ran his hands through his wet hair.

That kiss. That *kiss*.

It had been the most surprising, electric, erotic kiss of his life.

He'd always known there was more to Jessica than what most people saw, but even he would never have expected that.

The way she'd surged into him . . . He'd experienced some good kisses in his life, but nothing like that. The rain, the ocean . . . and Jessica, so unexpectedly passionate that he still couldn't believe he'd been able to control himself.

His wet shirt was starting to feel clammy. He unbuttoned it and pulled it off.

He'd done the right thing. She'd had even more alcohol than he'd thought at first, and she was vulnerable. So he'd made his offer: if she still felt the same way in the morning, they could do something about it.

It was an empty offer. He was one hundred percent certain that when Jessica woke up tomorrow, she wouldn't feel the same way. Which, in itself, was a reason to rein in his libido.

If he needed another reason, well . . . there was the fact that this was Jessica.

Jessica.

He'd made his share of mistakes with women, including a few one-night stands that had been the result of too much alcohol and too little judgment.

But Jessica wasn't some woman he'd met at a bar or a party. She was . . .

What the hell was she?

Not a friend, exactly. Not an enemy, either—not anymore.

He shook his head slowly. Whatever she was, he knew what she wasn't: a woman he could sleep with casually.

He scrubbed his face with his hands, leaned back, and shut his eyes.

Unfortunately, with his eyes closed, he was free to remember exactly how sexy Jessica had looked in that ocean tonight.

"You can't stargaze with your eyes shut."

He jerked upright. How in the hell had he missed the sound of the doorknob turning?

Jessica smiled at him from the doorway. She was wearing silky pajamas that clung to her slim curves as lovingly—if not quite as dramatically—as her soaking wet dress had. Her hair had been blown dry until it was silkier than her pjs, and her face was free of makeup.

And damn if he wasn't getting hard again.

But the fastest way to deal with that problem—and to put this night behind him—was to take a shower himself and go to bed. So he surged to his feet, grabbed his wet clothes, and went through the door Jess was holding open for him. Careful not to let himself look at her, he dropped his wet things in a pile by the closet, grabbed the sweats and T-shirt he planned to wear to bed, and headed for the bathroom.

The hot water felt good. He stood under the spray for longer than he needed to get clean, reminding himself of all the reasons to leave Jess alone tonight. He toweled himself off, pulled on his clothes, and went out into the bedroom as though wild animals might be lying in wait for him.

No wild animals, but there was definitely danger in the form of Jessica Bullock, all of five foot four and a hundred and ten pounds, lying in bed curled up on her side. It was a big bed and she was at the extreme right side of it, but the prospect of sliding under the covers with her—even if he was on the extreme left side—was too much for his peace of mind.

The light on her nightstand was off, but she'd left his on. Her eyes were closed, so he moved softly to turn off the light before heading for the sitting area.

"Where are you going?"

He froze. His eyes hadn't adjusted to the darkness yet, so he couldn't see Jessica's expression—only the fact that she was sitting up in bed.

"I'm going to sleep on the floor tonight," he said.

"That's silly. Are you afraid I'm going to ravish you or something?"

He couldn't help smiling. "No."

"Well, good. Because I have to wait for tomorrow morning to do that, so you don't have anything to worry about tonight. And this is a really big bed, so why don't you sleep here?"

She was sitting with her arms wrapped around her knees, and as his eyes adjusted to the darkness he could see her a little more clearly.

"You sure?"

"Of course I'm sure. But don't forget that come daybreak, you'll be at my mercy."

"I'll bear it in mind," he said, coming back to the bed and getting under the covers.

They lay in silence for a few minutes. He was on his back, but he could see Jessica out of the corner of his eye. She'd slid back under the covers herself and was lying on her side again, facing away from him.

He'd gotten up way too early that morning, and he was more than ready to fall asleep. So why was he keeping himself awake?

After a while he realized why. Because once he let himself slip into oblivion, it would be the end of this moment.

This moment when Jessica Bullock, whether because of alcohol or emotional vulnerability or a combination of the two, actually wanted to sleep with him.

He frowned up at the ceiling. Why would he want to hang on to that moment? Was it possible that he—

Suddenly frustrated with himself, he turned onto his left side and closed his eyes.

It took him less than a minute to fall asleep.

Chapter Eight

The sun was way too bright—like supernova bright. Was it possible the earth's star was expanding and would shortly explode?

Jessica rolled away from the glare and found herself face-to-face with Ben.

He was asleep, lying on his back with his head turned toward her, and for a moment all she could do was stare at him.

The shadow of stubble darkened his jaw, giving him a faintly piratical air. Without the warmth of his brown eyes to provide an intriguing contrast, the rough planes of his face seemed harsher than when he was awake.

His craggy features and well-muscled body projected hardness, power, and uncompromising determination. If you saw only what was on the outside, you'd think you were looking at a man who would take what he wanted without asking permission first. Only a glimpse of the soul behind that rough exterior would reveal the true story.

Ben Taggart was a gentleman.

Jessica squeezed her eyes shut, as though that could make the last twelve hours disappear.

Ben was a gentleman, all right. He'd proved it last night when she'd thrown herself at him . . . and he'd turned her down.

The more she tried not to remember, the more she remembered.

The two of them walking out into the ocean. The glory of the sea and the rain and the feeling of freedom surging through her veins.

And stronger than all of that, the pull she felt toward Ben.

He'd gone along with her crazy plan without hesitation, walking beside her through the pouring rain like a cheerful lunatic, and then following her into the ocean. His vigor and vitality seemed to flow into her until she felt as strong and fearless as he was.

Fearless enough to kiss him.

There'd been a time when she'd fantasized about kissing Ben Taggart. It came back to her now: the nights she'd lain awake thinking about him after days spent staying as far from him as she could.

You would have assumed from her behavior in school that she never wasted a thought on him. But at night she'd imagined his lips on hers, wondering what it would be like to kiss him.

Now, years later, she knew.

An explosion. Fireworks. A thousand sensations at once.

In the moments before he had pushed her away, she'd felt a wealth of carnal knowledge in his unerring touch. His mouth had fastened on hers with raw hunger.

When she felt the thick ridge of his erection pressed against her stomach, a thrill of excitement had set her nerve endings on fire. After spending the last few years thinking she was frigid and cold—maybe even asexual—the rush of erotic fire had been like a revelation.

Sober now and in the harsh light of day, she could hardly recognize the woman she'd been last night. She'd wrapped herself around Ben's hard body and kissed him as though the world might end at any moment.

If it had been up to her, they would have done the deed. Instead of lying here fully clothed, the two of them could be tangled up together in sweaty, sex-smelling sheets.

She sat up, wrapping her arms around her legs and resting her forehead on her knees.

A rogue part of her wished—oh, how she wished—that Ben wasn't such a gentleman. That she could have experienced, just once, honest-to-God passion in bed. It had been years since she'd dated, and none of her boyfriends had ever made her a feel a fraction of what Ben did.

Last night something inside her had broken free. But it was back in its cage now—and it was impossible to imagine setting it loose again.

That was why she almost wished Ben had taken advantage of the situation. But the bigger part of her—the sane part—was grateful that he was who he was.

"Morning."

She jerked her head up. Ben was on his side facing her, propped up on one elbow. His expression was quizzical, and he wore a slight smile.

Her mouth opened but she couldn't seem to speak. After a moment Ben's smile faded, replaced by a frown of concern.

"Are you okay?"

She had to answer. She couldn't go on staring at him like an imbecile.

"I'm fine," she managed to say, though her voice came out a little raspy. Dehydration from the hangover, no doubt.

Deciding she could better cope with the situation if she weren't in bed with him, she swung her legs toward the floor and started to get up. Unfortunately, her feet tangled in the covers and she went down on her butt.

"Jess?"

"I'm fine," she said again, her face beet red. She started to rise, tripped herself up again, and this time carefully unwound the blanket from her left foot. Then, with what shreds of dignity she could muster, she managed to stand.

Ben was sitting up, his expression carefully neutral—but there was a slight quirk at the corner of his mouth that told a different story.

"Everything good?" he asked.

"Of course," she replied stiffly. "Do you want the bathroom before me?"

"No, you can go first. Unless . . ."

"Unless what?"

The grin came out as Ben folded his arms behind his head and leaned back against his pillows. "I did promise that if you still lusted after me this morning, I'd do my best to satisfy you. How's your libido? Anything you'd like me to take care of before you start your day?"

Okay, so he wasn't a *perfect* gentleman. A perfect gentleman would have pretended last night had never happened.

"I'm all set, thanks," she said primly. She glanced at the clock. "It's after nine, so we should get a move on if we want breakfast. The buffet closes at ten."

Then she fled into the bathroom.

~

She'd been half afraid Ben would tease her at breakfast, but he kept the conversation light. By the time she'd finished her coffee and egg-white omelet, order had been restored in the form of a mutual decision to put last night behind them.

She breathed a sigh of relief as they left the buffet room.

"What are your plans for the day?" Ben asked.

"My plans?"

"That's right. You know, plans? The stuff you do in lieu of playing solitaire or staring off into space."

"I just . . . I mean . . . you said *my* plans. As in, my plans without you."

They pushed through the lobby doors to the porch, which reminded her of last night. This was where she'd stood watching the rain come down. Today, by contrast, was postcard beautiful—clean blue skies and a few puffy white clouds.

Ben grinned down at her. "Are you saying you want to spend the day with me?"

"I don't . . . I didn't mean . . ." She took a breath, wondering if her aplomb had deserted her forever or if it was a Ben-specific thing. "Of course you don't have to spend the day with me. I just wondered if you had plans of your own? It sounded like maybe you did."

"As a matter of fact, I do. Since I'm deprived my regular sports, I thought I'd go check out some cricket."

"Are you serious?"

"Why not? Apparently today and tomorrow are the Bermuda World Series of cricket. And the game—"

"It's called a match."

"—the match lasts all day, with food and rum and gambling and music. I'm definitely up for that."

Jessica had dated an Australian businessman once who loved cricket, and who had persuaded her to sit through something he'd called the Ashes.

"Cricket makes no sense. Nothing at all happens for a long time, and then a ball gets hit and someone runs back and forth for no apparent reason. After three hours or so the score is 195 to zero and you think that's it, stick a fork in it, but then the team that was at zero goes on to win. I don't think you'll enjoy it."

"Are you kidding? It sounds great. Let's go."

The sun was in her eyes, and she lifted a hand to shade them as she looked up at Ben. "Let's go? As in, both of us?"

"Unless you've got something else going on. It's not dolphin day, is it?"

She shook her head. "That's tomorrow."

"Well, then, there you go. Why not come with me? It's a gorgeous day, and it sounds like the cricket match is just an excuse for a big party. Let's go check it out. The best way to learn about a culture is at its favorite sporting event. What do you say?"

"Well . . ."

He grinned. "Great. I'll meet you out front in a few minutes, okay? There's something I want to pick up at the gift shop."

Should she go back to the room? She was wearing a pair of blue capri pants and a white shirt with spaghetti straps. Did she need to change? No—a cricket match wouldn't require anything more formal.

She wandered back through the lobby, stopping at the cricket display the hotel staff had helpfully set up. Shaking her head at the oddly shaped bat and ball, it occurred to her that she could have opted to do something else—shop in Hamilton's boutique district, wander through the four-hundred-year-old town of St. George, sit by the pool or swim in the ocean or—well, anything. But for some reason, in spite of last night's embarrassing debacle, she still wanted to spend time with Ben more than she wanted to do any of those things.

Which, today, meant going to a cricket match.

She went out through the front doors and waited for Ben. He came out a few minutes later, carrying a bag from the gift shop.

"Here," he said, pulling out two T-shirts. "Pick a team."

"A team?"

"Somerset or St. George."

"I don't understand."

"Those are the two teams playing today," he explained patiently. "The St. George players are from the east side of the island, and the Somerset players are from the west. They play each other once a year."

She looked at the T-shirts he was holding up. "Let me get this straight. You want us to wear the T-shirts of the two cricket teams?"

"Sure. The staff here at the hotel seem equally divided between the two, so they told me it was good that we'd be representing both sides."

"The locals don't mind when tourists wear these things? I mean, I know Yankees fans would absolutely hate it if a bunch of tourists from another country showed up at a game wearing pinstripes."

"It happens all the time, and yeah, New Yorkers hate that. But in case you haven't noticed, Bermudians are a lot more friendly. It'll be fine, Jess. Just pick a shirt."

The St. George colors were light blue and dark blue; the Somerset colors were dark blue and red.

"I guess I'll go with this one," she said, reaching for the St. George shirt.

"Perfect," Ben said, exchanging his plain tee for the Somerset one.

Jessica pulled her new T-shirt on over what she was wearing. It was enormous, the sleeves down nearly to her elbows and the hem falling to the middle of her thighs.

"I can't wear this," she said. "I look ridiculous."

"You look fine," Ben said firmly, steering her across the driveway toward the main road. "They're running low on shirts, and there aren't any smaller sizes in stock."

"You passed the taxi stand," Jessica said, trying to stop.

Ben shook his head and kept going. "We're taking the bus."

"The bus?"

"Yep. It'll be more fun."

"What'll be fun about it?"

That question was answered a few minutes later when they took their seats among the raucous locals riding to the cricket stadium.

Jessica had never seen such a happy group of people in her life. Most of them were wearing the dark blue and light blue of St. George, and they seemed to regard Jessica as a long-lost cousin.

"St. George!" they cried out when they saw her.

"Sit here by me," an elderly woman said, patting the seat next to her. "Your husband can stand, since he's for the wrong team."

"He's not my husband, and I'm not really a fan," she said anxiously, feeling like she was receiving friendliness under false pretenses. "He only bought these shirts for us this morning. I don't know anything about the team."

The woman, who was dressed head to toe in the St. George colors—including an enormous straw hat bedecked in light and dark blue ribbons—just laughed. "Well, then. At least you've started by picking the right side."

The bus ride took twenty minutes, which gave Jessica time to listen to the chatter of the people around her. They were engaged in passionate discussions about the minutiae of the match they were about to attend. Whenever she caught Ben's eye, he was smiling, which made her realize she was smiling, too.

Even though she had little idea what they were talking about, she found herself caught up in the enthusiasm. Before the ride was over, she agreed to a young girl's suggestion to tie back her hair with a St. George ribbon.

"Very nice," Ben said as they got off the bus and went toward the line of people snaking out from the stadium ticket booth.

"I couldn't say no. That little girl was so adorable."

"You're pretty adorable, too."

She was taken off guard, but Ben reached the ticket booth just then, so she didn't have to answer.

He thought she was adorable?

She was surprised at how good it felt to hear that. But was her pleasure because of the compliment, or the person who'd given it to her?

No. For once in her life, she wasn't going to second-guess herself. She was going to follow Ben's example and enjoy this beautiful day in the company of thousands of people doing the same thing.

Once they got inside, they found that the stadium was crowded. Tall bleachers enclosed the playing field and every seat seemed to be full. There were hundreds more people standing between the seats or milling around behind them, in the fairgrounds surrounding the stadium.

She and Ben wandered for a little while, hearing the cheers first of the St. George fans and then the Somerset fans without being able to see the match.

"I guess we won't find a seat," Jessica said after a few minutes. "Maybe we should just—"

"We'll find a seat," Ben said confidently, grabbing her hand. "I just spotted a friend."

He led her through the crowd to a section of the stands that had been roped off.

"Juliette!" he called out, grinning at the woman they'd met on the bus. She was manning a table with a dozen pitchers of some fruity-looking beverage.

"Well, hello there!" she said, pouring some of the drink into two plastic cups and handing them across the table. "If it isn't the young married couple that isn't really a married couple. You know there's a section on the far side that's just for tourists?"

"Oh," Jessica said quickly, feeling like an interloper. "I'm sorry, we—"

"Luckily for you, you won't have to sit with them. Come on back here with me." She came out from behind the table, calling out, "Take over for me a minute, Fred."

Clutching her plastic cup and hoping she didn't spill whatever it was, she followed Juliette into a dark space under a section of bleachers until they came out into a bright patch right on the edge of the action. A handful of Bermudians—in St. George garb, she was happy to see—were sitting on lawn chairs.

"These are friends of mine," Juliette said to them. "The girl's got her head on right, but this boy has sadly been led astray. They're from America and need some kind soul to explain the game to them."

They called out their thanks as Juliette hurried away, and an elderly man and a woman who turned out to be his daughter pulled their chairs close and started giving a play-by-play of the action on the field.

Jessica took a cautious sip of her mysterious drink and tasted fruit juices and alcohol.

"It's a rum swizzle," Ben said, leaning close to be heard over a sudden roar of approval for something or other.

"A rum swizzle? But it's not even noon yet. Isn't it a little early for alcohol?"

"Think of it as fruit juice with a kick," Ben said, taking a healthy swallow of his. "And considering we're going to be watching cricket for the next several hours, I'd give some serious consideration to getting sozzled. It might make the game—sorry, match—seem more comprehensible."

"Fair point," Jessica said, taking another and bigger sip of her own drink.

Having one rum swizzle was one thing. But when Juliette came over with a pitcher and refilled her cup, she hesitated.

She'd only just recovered from last night's hangover with the help of water and Advil. She still hadn't entirely recovered from the embarrassment of her behavior. Alcohol was going to play no part in the rest of her vacation—or at least, no more than a glass of wine with dinner.

Ben saw her frowning down at her newly filled cup and grinned. He leaned close again, close enough that she caught a whiff of soap and sun-warmed skin.

"Afraid you'll try to kiss me again if you have another?"

A rush of heat went through her—equal parts embarrassment and something else she didn't want to identify.

"Of course not," she said with dignity, taking a sip to prove her point.

As the hours passed and the game—match—wore on, she found herself leaping to her feet with the other St. George fans when one of their batsmen hit one to the boundary or one of their fielders made a spectacular defensive play.

"In your *face*," she said to Ben with a grin as their score mounted in the fifth inning. "You know, it's not too late for you to switch allegiances. We're not too proud to take you in."

"Yes, we are!" one of their new friends called out.

"No, we're not," another one contradicted—a young woman who'd shown a lot of interest in Ben once she learned that he wasn't "with" Jessica.

He shook his head sadly. "I'm no fair-weather fan. Once for Somerset, always for Somerset."

At some point—Jessica had lost count of how many rum swizzles she'd had and was a little hazy as to details—Ben grabbed her hand and pulled her to her feet.

"Come on," he said, leading her back through the throng and toward a tent in the fields beyond the green.

"What's in here?"

"Apparently gambling is illegal in Bermuda except for one two-day period."

"The Cup Match?"

"The Cup Match."

"But I don't gamble," she objected as she and Ben ducked under the shade of the tent and into happy chaos—dozens of tables scattered around with crowds of shouting, laughing people clustered around each.

"Neither do I—and neither does Bermuda, except for today. I was told we have to give it a try."

They worked their way close to the action at one of the tables, but though Jessica tried to make sense of the grids marked on the tables and the passing of money back and forth, she had absolutely no idea what was going on.

"It's called crown-and-anchor," Ben said in her ear, and she shivered. She hadn't realized he was so close.

"I don't know what people are betting on."

"Me neither, to be honest. But we should definitely have a flutter." He opened his wallet and pulled out a five-dollar bill, placing it on one of the squares on the table. Some mysterious things happened and then there was another five on top of their first one.

"You won!" she cried out, delighted, and Ben grinned down at her.

"We won," he corrected her. "Should we keep going?"

"Yes!"

They won again, and then again. She still had no idea what was going on, but she was almost certain she'd never had so much fun in her life.

Even when they lost it all on the next throw, she still thought so.

"It's a good thing they only do this once a year," she said as she and Ben wandered out to the fairgrounds. "Come to think of it, that's not a bad system. I mean, it's hard to become an addict or ruin your life if you can only gamble once a year."

"I'm glad to know I haven't led you down a path of irresistible temptation," Ben said, squeezing her hand.

She hadn't actually realized he was holding her hand until that moment.

She was surprised at how right it felt—so right she hadn't even questioned it.

Of course, she was also well past tipsy and on her way to truly inebriated . . . for the third time in three days.

As the afternoon wore on, Jessica focused half her attention on the match and the other half on a burning question.

Would the world come to an end if she kissed Ben again?

More importantly, would he reject her if she did? Or would he . . .

She closed her eyes as her imagination took over.

"You're not falling asleep on me, I hope," he said in her ear.

God, she loved it when he leaned close and whispered like that. His breath against her skin made her shiver, and the warmth of his nearness made her feel safe and excited at the same time.

A little while later, as they were wending their way through the crowd toward the exit—they'd decided to leave before the day's match was over to avoid a crush of people all leaving at once—she heard herself ask, "What would you do if I kissed you again?"

Of course it couldn't be her who'd asked that question. That wouldn't be like her at all, and—

Ben had stopped walking, and she stopped too.

"Oh my God. I said that out loud, didn't I?"

Ben put his arm around her shoulders as they started walking again, toward the bus stop on the side of the road.

"You did," he said. "But we can pretend you didn't, if that's what you want."

"I—" She stopped and started again. "I—"

They reached the bus stop and sat down in the shade of the shelter. It was plastered over with flyers and St. George signs, and it smelled the way you'd expect a bus stop to smell, and it occurred to Jessica that she couldn't have chosen a less likely location for a seduction . . . if that's what she was doing.

But that was the thing. She didn't know what she was doing.

"If I didn't want to forget I said it, what would *you* say?" she asked.

As the words came out of her mouth, it occurred to her that a more cowardly pass had never been made . . . if she was making a pass.

Was she making a pass?

Oh God, she was making a pass. Ineptly, but still. A pass was being made. By her.

"Hedging your bets, huh?" Ben asked.

A foot of space separated them on the concrete bench.

She felt her color rising. "I'm not very good at this," she said after a moment.

He held up a hand. "Hey, I wasn't criticizing your moves. Men struggle with this from the age of fourteen, and frankly, we should all be grateful for the women brave enough to wade out into the fray. I was just teasing you because it's fun to tease you . . . and because I've had such a great time with you today."

"You have?"

"Of course I have. Wasn't it obvious?"

Nothing was obvious to her. Her understanding of human signals—at least when it came to man-woman signals—had gotten screwed up somewhere along the line.

But that wasn't going to stop her this time.

"Ben—"

He held up a hand again. "I haven't answered your question yet."

"My question?"

"About what I would say if you asked me to kiss you."

"Oh." She paused. "What *would* you say?"

"For starters, I would say that I've been fighting the urge to kiss you all day."

Warmth spread through her. "You *have?*"

"How can you be surprised? You're one of the sexiest women I've ever known."

"You think I'm *sexy?*"

"Hell yes, I think you're sexy."

She looked down at herself. "But I'm a mess. This shirt is three sizes too big, and I've spilled food and rum swizzle all over it, and I smell like cheap sunscreen and—"

"Jessica."

She blinked up at him. "Yes?"

Ben's eyes were surprisingly serious.

"Please don't ever doubt how sexy you are. I've been imagining what it would be like to slide my hands under that T-shirt all day. I've been remembering last night, too, and feeling like the world's biggest idiot for turning you down." He took a breath. "And I'm going to have to do it again, because this time, *I'm* drunk. But, Jessica, if you ever want to ask me that question when we're both sober . . . the answer will be hell yes."

She frowned down at her shoes. It was the nicest rejection she'd ever heard, but it was still a rejection.

"But what if it's hard?" She swallowed. "I mean . . . what if I can't ask you unless I've been drinking?"

He cocked his head to the side and studied her for a moment. "Why would it be hard?"

The alcohol in her system was loosening her tongue, lifting her inhibitions. She realized that she was actually close to telling him what made it so hard.

That realization, more than anything else, was enough to sober her up a little.

She didn't say anything. She looked at Ben, and he looked at her. And then, thank God, their bus came rumbling down the road.

~

The moment was past—again. Was every day in Bermuda going to come with these temptations? The temptation to set aside chivalry and whatever the hell else was stopping him from acting on his instincts?

He had the bathroom first when they got back to their cottage. They were eating at the hotel's informal restaurant tonight, so after he showered and shaved he put on a pair of khakis and a polo shirt.

When Jessica came out of the bathroom, he had to catch his breath. She looked fresh and sweet and lovely. She was wearing a light blue dress, very simple, and she'd tied a navy blue scarf around her throat.

After a moment he realized the significance of her choice.

"You're wearing St. George colors," he said with a sudden grin.

"They're playing again tomorrow," she reminded him.

"I know."

A few minutes later, strolling up the flagstone path to the main building, Ben tried to identify the feeling that kept creeping into his consciousness as he walked beside Jessica.

And then, with an uncomfortable shock, he realized what it was.

It was the first-date feeling.

Which, of course, made no sense on any level.

This wasn't a date, for one thing. And even if it were, it wouldn't be their first.

But neither of those very obvious truths made the feeling go away. That subtle desire to protect, to impress, to brush up against her at every opportunity.

Not to mention the slow burn of desire running through his veins.

A few hours had gone by since they'd had their last rum swizzle. If they avoided alcohol during dinner, would that satisfy his criteria for sobriety?

He let Jessica precede him into the lobby and shook his head. A sober Jessica, he felt sure, would retreat to the safe and predictable. Fooling around with him was a temptation that came over her while she was under the influence. In her right mind, she'd always think better of any random desires she experienced when she was drinking.

But there was nothing stopping him from eying her curves as she walked in front of him, or admiring the subtle sway of her hips.

The first-date feeling carried over into dinner. Everything felt different, and not just because they both drank iced tea instead of wine or cocktails. He was aware of the candlelight that illuminated their table and the way it flattered Jessica's creamy skin. She wore her hair down, the soft blonde waves moving like water over her bare shoulders. When she bent her head toward her plate, a strand would fall forward, and every time she tucked it behind her ear he wished he could do that for her.

They talked about cricket and rum and gambling, and the music and dancing they'd seen when they went to the food tents for lunch.

It wasn't just a first date. It was one of the best first dates he'd ever had.

No, he reminded himself. *Not* a first date. Dinner with an old friend who was going through a rough time.

They'd finished their entrees. Jessica was sitting with her elbow on the table and her chin in her hand, gazing out the window. It was a clear night, and the crescent moon, a little bigger this evening than last, hung in the sky above the ocean.

He remembered the way she'd looked earlier that day, sitting at the bus stop. She'd been relaxed and happy until the moment she'd (sort of) propositioned him. But then her expression had changed, almost as though she was haunted by something.

What if I can't ask you unless I've been drinking? What if it's hard?

Why would it be hard to ask for what she wanted when she was sober? To kiss him when she was sober?

Maybe it wasn't only about Jessica's fear of acting on her impulses. Maybe there was something else going on, something beneath the surface. Something that didn't have anything to do with him at all.

Something that was none of his business.

CHAPTER NINE

The next day, he got to see Jessica swim with dolphins.

He'd had a restless night. Jessica's delicate scent had floated toward him from her side of the bed, and it was hard to lie beside her without pulling her into his arms. His body craved hers, and he was starting to think sleeping on the floor might—ironically—be a more comfortable option.

Eventually he'd fallen asleep. When he woke, Jessica was already up and dressed.

He sat up in bed and dragged a hand through his hair. "Morning."

"Good morning." She came over and sat on the edge of the bed. "You know," she began—and then she stopped.

"Yeah?" he asked after a moment, wondering what had happened to the rest of the sentence.

"Well. You know this is my day with dolphins?"

"Uh-huh."

"Well," she said again. "Tom was interested in seeing the program, so when I reserved my spot, I asked if he could watch part of it. They said he could observe the last half hour. I thought . . . if you're interested . . ."

"Sure," he said.

Her face lit up. "Really? You won't think it's silly?"

"Even if I did, I wouldn't say so after dragging you to an eight-hour cricket match. But as a matter of fact, I don't think it's silly. I'd love to go."

"Well, then. That's great." She reached into her bag and pulled out a few printed sheets. "Here's your information, where to go and what to do and all that." She paused. "So I guess I'll see you there."

"See you there."

A few minutes later, the door closed behind her and he had the suite to himself. He made coffee and spent some time with his smartphone, catching up on email and social media.

But it was hard to concentrate when thoughts of Jessica kept popping up. The way her hair shone in the sun . . . the way she'd looked at dinner last night . . . that kiss in the ocean.

He also remembered the girl who'd preferred animals to people and who'd worn a dolphin necklace all through sixth grade.

When she was ten, she'd started giving her birthday money to the Wildlife Foundation. They had a program where you could symbolically "adopt" an animal species, and Jessica had asked friends and family to donate in her name in lieu of Christmas gifts. The walls of her bedroom had been covered with pictures of tigers and polar bears and elephants—and, of course, dolphins.

Bermuda's dolphin program took place on the western part of the island, and the quickest way to get there was by ferry from Hamilton. Ben took a bus into town and bought his ticket. As the boat motored away from the dock, he found himself recalling a short story Jessica had written for English class once. It was about a mermaid whose best friend was a dolphin.

The memory made him smile. Even if this was the only thing she got out of her trip, he was very glad she'd decided to go.

The dolphins—there were a dozen of them, according to the sheet Jessica had given him—lived in an enclosed lagoon. When he arrived at the program office, they directed him out to the habitat.

After he sat down on a bench near the edge of the water, he saw Jessica and someone else—a trainer, he assumed—come out of a low building on the other side of the lagoon. They were chatting away like old friends, and Jessica was carrying a bucket of . . .

Fish?

Of course, it made sense that a day with dolphins would include fish at some point. But somehow, he would never have expected to see Jessica carrying a bucketful of them.

There was a wooden dock extending out into the middle of the lagoon. Jessica and the other woman, both wearing black bathing suits and red floating vests, sat down with their legs dangling over the side. Suddenly a smooth gray head—no, two—popped up in the water.

Jessica and the other woman held out their hands, and the dolphins swam closer—close enough for the two women to hold their heads and kiss their noses.

Noses? Was that the right term?

After the kisses, they held their hands higher up and farther apart, which apparently was the signal for the dolphins to come farther up out of the water, offering their fins to their human companions. For a few minutes the women held on to the dolphins' fins in a kind of dance, and then the dolphins dipped back down into the water before coming up again.

Now Jessica reached into the bucket, pulled out two fish, and tossed them to her friends.

Not only had she carried a bucketful of fish, but now she was getting her hands dirty—not to mention smelly—with them.

And Ben had never seen her happier.

He'd seen flashes of pleasure in Jess during the past few days, but this was something else. She'd had fun at the cricket match yesterday, but this was pure joy.

He leaned forward, captivated. She was eager, enthusiastic, alive, with a smile that lit up her face like sunshine.

She should look like this all the time.

Then she turned her head and caught sight of him, and her face glowed even brighter. She waved at him and he waved back.

The trainer said something to her, and then Jessica slid into the water. She started to swim, accompanied by one of the dolphins, and the two of them seemed alike somehow—fast and graceful and full of joy. Ben decided he could never get tired of watching Jessica like this.

In her element.

Ten minutes later the program ended and Jessica went into the building to change. When she reappeared in her shorts and T-shirt, her wet hair braided down her back, she came hurrying over to him.

"Hey," she said breathlessly. "Oh, I'm so glad you came. It was a wonderful day." She smiled up at him, still glowing.

"I can tell," he said. An impulse made him take her hand as they left the lagoon area and headed for the exit.

She didn't seem to mind—or maybe she was too happy to notice. "I didn't think the experience would live up to my expectations," she said. "Nothing ever does, right? But it was even better than I thought it would be. Do you know dolphins are right behind humans in terms of brain size? When you interact with them, you really feel their intelligence. Their personality. They're so playful . . ."

She continued talking as they made their way to the ferry, with him asking questions whenever she paused for breath. After they'd boarded the boat and taken seats in the bow, he said to her, "You should do this."

They were sitting side by side, and he still held her hand in his. The ferry pulled away from the dock and the breeze picked up, tugging a strand of pale blonde hair out of Jessica's braid.

She tucked it behind her ear. "Do what?"

"Something with dolphins, or the ocean, or animals. You could buy a boat and sail around the world. Or go back to school and study marine biology like you always wanted. Or you could join the ASPCA, or become a veterinarian."

She kept her eyes forward, not looking at him. "Just like that, huh?"

He squeezed her hand. "Not just like that. I know it won't be easy to figure out your next steps. But you're smart and you're passionate, and when you're doing something you love, you're like a bolt of pure energy. That light is going to make the world a better place, Jess. You just have to figure out how you want to focus it."

She was still looking out at the water. "How is someone like me going to make the world a better place?"

"Are you kidding?" He shifted on the bench and took her shoulders, pulling her around to face him. "All you have to do is be yourself. The woman I just saw swimming with dolphins will make the world a better place. You just have to decide how. What do you have to lose?"

She stared at him. "I don't—I've never—" She shook her head. "That's not how I live my life."

"I know. But don't you think it's time to make a change?" He paused. "That night at the reception, you said you felt empty. But it doesn't have to be that way. Your goal used to be meeting other people's expectations. Fitting in, making your parents happy, satisfying someone else's standards of good behavior. But that can be part of your past. Starting right now, this very minute, you can decide to take a different path. Even if it's hard, even if it seems crazy, you can decide to do something you love."

For a long moment they just looked at each other. Ben kept his hands on Jessica's shoulders, wanting her to feel the warmth and solidity of another person's presence. Wanting her to know she wasn't alone.

Finally she took a deep breath and let it out slowly. "I wouldn't know where to start."

He smiled. "Why don't you do what you did when you were a kid? Make a list. Write down all the things you could do with your life, even if they sound impossible. Start there. Then narrow it down to the things that make you feel the most alive, the most excited, the most happy. Then make new lists, lists of the steps you'd need to take to get there."

Jessica looked at him, and he got the feeling she wasn't thinking about her own life anymore.

He got the feeling she was thinking about him.

"Is this how you talk to your students?" she asked. "No wonder they love you."

He shook his head. "They don't all love me. These are teenagers we're talking about."

She smiled. "I know about your Teacher of the Year award. Remember?"

He brushed that off. "We're not talking about me right now. We're talking about you—and all the new lists you're going to make."

"I'll think about it. Okay? That's the best I can do right now."

"All right," he said, taking his hands from her shoulders. "I can live with that."

They sat in silence for a moment, looking out at the ocean and feeling the wind on their faces. The sun, behind them, struck golden sparks off the blue water.

"I'm sorry if I got intense," he said after a minute. "When I saw how happy you were today . . ." He shook his head. "I wish you could look like that all the time."

"I know."

There was an undercurrent in her voice he didn't understand. He turned his head, and she was looking straight ahead with an odd look on her face.

"What are you thinking about?" he asked.

When she met his eyes, he noticed that hers were the color of the sea. "I'm making a list in my head," she said. "Just like you suggested. Things I could do to make me feel alive, and what I need to do to get there."

~

They arrived back at the hotel a couple of hours before dinner.

Ben seemed a little restless. "I think I'm going to check out the hotel fitness center," he said. "Do you want to come?"

Jessica shook her head. "I might do some snorkeling later. I rented gear for you, too, if you're interested."

"Yeah, that probably won't happen. Snorkeling's not my thing. I tried to breathe with one of those masks on once and it felt claustrophobic."

Jessica sat down on the bed and smiled at him. "That's because you have control issues."

He was fishing around in one of the bureau drawers for work-out clothes, but now he straightened up and stared at her. "What are you talking about? I don't have control issues."

"I know, I know—I'm the one with control issues. That's the story, right? And yes, I definitely have them. But you've never admitted that you have them, too."

"That's because I don't," he said firmly.

"Uh-huh. Don't you remember when I taught you to swim? It took me weeks to convince you to put your head in the water. And the only reason I was teaching you in the first place was because you refused to take lessons when you were little. Your parents practically begged me to get you in the pool."

"That's not because I had control issues. I had water issues. And I've gotten over them."

Jessica reached down beside the bed, grabbed one of the snorkel masks she'd rented, and held it up.

"Okay, I've mostly gotten over them. When did you become such an expert on this stuff, anyway?"

"Because of all my control issues," Jessica said. "I recognize the signs."

"I see." Ben grinned at her. "Well, I'm still not going snorkeling with you."

"Snorkeling to you is like dessert for me. I let you talk me into having that sundae, didn't I?"

"You only had one bite. And hot fudge sundaes are way more tempting than snorkeling."

"You only say that because you've never been. I'm telling you, it's wonderful."

"Not as wonderful as ice cream."

"You can't say that until you've tried both."

"Man, you're persistent. I think I'm going to end this argument the old-fashioned way—by going to the gym." He stuffed his workout clothes into a bag and headed for the door, pausing with his hand on the knob. "See you later, Jess."

Once he was gone, Jessica went to the window to watch him stride up the path toward the hotel. As her eyes followed him until he was out of sight, she found herself smiling.

Something had happened to her on that ferry this afternoon. The joy the dolphins had sparked in her had combined with the joy of being around Ben until it felt like she was lit from within. Never in her life had she felt like that—like she had access to enough joy to drive out every last bit of darkness inside her.

She remembered the intensity in Ben's brown eyes when he'd looked at her on the ferry, pouring out his faith in the human spir-it—his faith in *her*—as though his own conviction and certainty could overcome her lack of those things. As though he could fuel her with his strength and courage and vitality.

And it had worked. Just like that night at the reception, she'd felt possibility ignite within her. That night, it had been the possi-bility of taking her honeymoon trip without Tom, of spending ten days doing things just because she wanted to. Today, it was the pos-sibility that she might have something to contribute to the world. The possibility of a meaningful future. A future doing something she loved—even if she wasn't quite sure what that would be.

But before she could tackle that enormous task, there was something else she wanted to do.

Because Ben was right. She could choose a different path. She could choose to live a life of passion.

Including sexual passion.

For too long she'd settled for relationships without it. Sex had always been something she'd done because it was expected, not because she enjoyed it.

It wasn't that she hated it. It had always felt okay, if not spec-tacular. Sometimes she'd feel turned on and start to think that may-be, finally, she'd be able to experience the physical passion that her friends talked about. But inevitably, at some point, her excitement would fade into a kind of detachment.

She'd decided a while ago that sexual ecstasy would never be part of her life. But now, for the first time, the possibility of physical passion felt real.

And it was something she wanted. Not just when she was drunk and acting on impulse, when she could tell herself afterward that she wasn't responsible for her actions. She could *choose* passion. She could choose to be with a man who made her feel alive.

She could choose to be with Ben.

She'd wanted him since before she understood what that meant, and tonight she was going to have him.

But the thought of seducing him felt impossible. The thought of kissing him when she was sober was terrifying. She had so much baggage when it came to sex . . . there was no way she could pretend she was a normal woman with a normal, healthy sexuality. Not without alcohol, anyway.

There was really only one solution. She would tell Ben what she needed in a clear, coherent way, and ask for his help. And while that approach might be completely unsexy, she was sure—say ninety percent sure—that he wouldn't turn her down.

He had a savior complex, after all. He loved to fix people.

And she was a woman who needed fixing.

~

She thought about suggesting room service for dinner instead of the restaurant, but talking to Ben in a public setting might actually make the conversation easier. She'd be less inclined to give way to embarrassing emotion, and more likely to make her case in a straightforward manner.

She dressed in navy-blue slacks and a sleeveless white blouse. She put her hair up and kept her makeup simple, the way she would at a business meeting.

She asked the maître d' if they could have a table in a quiet corner. Once they were seated, she glanced around, determining that the nearest diners weren't close enough to hear their conversation. She waited until the waiter had taken their order, and then folded her hands on the table.

"So," she said. "There's something I want to talk to you about."

She kept her voice casual, even businesslike. It was all in the presentation, she'd decided. She would sound like a rational woman who'd come to a decision about solving a problem.

"So you said on the way here." He imitated her posture, folding his hands and placing them on the table. "Are you looking for legal advice?"

She cleared her throat. "Neither of us has had any alcohol today."

Ben nodded gravely. "That's true. Does this mean you're planning to seduce me?"

His tone was teasing, since nothing about the atmosphere or their dynamic resembled a seduction scenario. But that couldn't be helped. She had to do it this way, at least in the beginning.

"Yes," she said.

He blinked. "Okay, I think I'm missing something."

"You are. Let me explain."

She paused. She'd rehearsed this so carefully, planned what she would say and how she would say it. But now that it had come to the point, the words stuck in her throat.

"I have something to tell you, but I need to do this a certain way. Will you promise not to say anything until I've finished? I need you to just sit and listen. Can you do that?"

"Of course," he said after a moment, looking puzzled. "Whatever you need."

"Okay. Good."

She couldn't do this while looking at him, so she looked down at her hands instead.

"So." She paused. "So."

Her heart was pounding and her stomach was in knots. But somehow, some way, she had to get through this.

What happens in Bermuda stays in Bermuda, she reminded herself. After this trip, she and Ben never had to see each other again.

"Okay. So." She squeezed her hands into fists and took a deep breath. "I have a problem with sex."

Silence.

After a moment she risked a glance up. Ben's brown eyes were opaque and his expression was neutral, and she couldn't tell what he was thinking. But he was listening and he wasn't laughing at her. So far so good.

She looked down at the table again. "I'm not a virgin or anything. I mean, I've had sex, but it's hard for me to . . . enjoy it. In fact, I don't. At least, I never have." She took a breath. "After a while I got tired of boyfriends calling me frigid or deciding I must be cheating on them or just losing interest, and I stopped dating. But when you don't date, your friends and family wonder what's wrong, and they try to fix you up with guys they think would be perfect for you, and . . . well, I got tired of that, too. So that's why I . . ."

"Got engaged to Tom?"

She glanced up quickly, but Ben didn't look or sound like he was judging her. She took a deep breath and went on, but this time she kept her eyes on his.

"Yes. Of course, there were a lot of other reasons for that decision. But one of them, for me, was this problem. With sex. I was tired of dealing with it, and the potential reward didn't seem worth the investment, to be honest. So I was glad to be out of all that. But now . . . now that the marriage isn't happening . . . I thought that maybe . . ."

Just get it out there. What's the worst that can happen?

"I thought maybe it's not too late. To have a normal sex life. When I get back to New York, you know? Since marrying a gay man didn't work out for me," she added, trying for a little humor. "I want . . . I just want . . . I want to know what it's like. To have good sex. To feel what other women feel."

She paused, searching Ben's eyes to discern his reaction.

It was so hard to read what he was thinking. But he wasn't judging her, and he wasn't laughing at her. That would have to be enough to go on with.

"So I wondered if you might . . . be willing . . . to help me."

A quick spasm went through her, but it was out. It was out, damn it, and the world hadn't ended.

She took a deep breath. "The other night, when we kissed, I felt . . . I mean . . . I don't usually feel like that. I've never wanted someone like I wanted you."

Her cheeks burned. But she needed to think about this clinically, like a conversation with a doctor. If this was going to work, Ben had to have all the information.

"Of course I've felt desire before, but . . . there's always been this disconnect. Once things start heating up I always freeze, or something. So I thought . . . this time . . . maybe I could take a more direct approach. If you know I have a problem, then you won't expect . . . that is, you won't be disappointed if . . . if things don't go well."

She cleared her throat. "You said I can figure out who I am by figuring out what I like. That's what I want to do. With you. With sex. And since you're moving to Chicago in the fall, there won't be any, you know, emotional fallout. You don't have to worry that I'm going to expect anything from you or get my heart broken or . . ."

She trailed off, seeing the waiter approaching with her salad and Ben's soup.

Maybe having this conversation in the restaurant had been a mistake. How was she supposed to eat?

She looked down at her plate. They'd put the dressing on the side. She focused on picking up the little silver pitcher and pouring the vinaigrette over her greens, and then she speared a bite and brought it to her mouth.

"Jessica?"

She choked on a slice of cucumber.

Oh God. She was coughing like she'd never stop.

Ben started to rise from his seat, but she waved him off. She gulped down some water, took a few deep breaths, and looked up.

"I'm sorry," she said. "You were saying something?"

God, what a disaster. What in the world had she been thinking?

"My answer is yes."

She stared at him for a long moment. His brown eyes were warm and alive, and the slight smile he wore didn't seem to be mocking her.

"It is?"

"Yeah."

Okay, then.

As she continued to sit there, her face getting hotter and hotter, it occurred to her that she hadn't thought past this point.

"What happens now?" she blurted.

Smooth, Jessica. Very smooth. All in all, this had to be the strangest—and least sexy—proposition a woman had ever made to a man.

"I don't know about you, but I'm going to eat dinner." He took a sip of his seafood chowder and made an appreciative noise. "Wow, that's good. Do you want to try this?"

He looked completely at ease, which was more than she could say for herself.

"You don't think it's weird to just sit here having dinner?"

He shook his head. "Nope. And we're not just having dinner. We're on a date, and it's my job to entertain you, to charm you, to give you the impression that I'm a responsible adult, and, hopefully, convince you to make out with me at the end of the night."

"But we're not really on a date. And you already know I want to make out."

Ben leaned toward her. "Do you trust me, Jess?"

Something in his expression told her that this was a serious question—one that could define the events going forward. So instead of answering quickly—*yes, of course I trust you*—she took a moment to think about it.

"I would trust you with my life."

He looked startled.

After a moment he cleared his throat. "Well, then. Will you trust me tonight? Enough to put yourself in my hands?"

This time she didn't hesitate. "Yes."

He nodded. "Good. Then we're on a date, which means I'm doing all the work. Your job is to enjoy yourself and let me know how I'm doing." He paused. "I'm going to start with something easy. How's your salad?"

She'd spit out the only bite she'd taken so far. Now she took another one. "It's very good."

"Excellent. You already know my soup is good. Are you ready for my next dating move?"

She was starting to relax a little. How could she not, when Ben was narrating the evening so disarmingly?

"I'm ready."

"You look beautiful tonight."

Her cheeks warmed. "Well, thank you. But I didn't do anything special. I mean . . . I didn't dress up or anything."

"You don't have to. You're Grace Kelly beautiful, Jess. You'd be gorgeous in a burlap sack."

She blushed deeper. "Okay, that's pretty good. I give you high marks for your dating moves so far." She took another bite of salad. "May I ask you a question?"

"Of course."

"It might be a bad date question."

"One of the rules for the evening is that you can do no wrong. Ask me whatever you want."

"All right." She cleared her throat. "You're a pretty nice guy, and not exactly hard to look at. How is it that you're still single?"

His eyebrows went up. "You're saying I'm easy on the eyes?"

Considering she'd been on the point of dissolving in embarrassment a few minutes ago, it was hard to believe they were actually joking now. "I'm not going to repeat it, if that's what you're angling for. Your ego doesn't need any stroking."

He nodded thoughtfully. "I guess that's true. After all, I'm the one you turned to when you needed a sex god."

"A sex god? Wow. You're setting the bar pretty high, aren't you? Most men would fold under that kind of pressure."

"I'm not most men."

She rolled her eyes. "Are you going to answer the question, or what?"

He paused as a waiter cleared their dishes and another set down their main course. "I was in a long-term relationship until about a year ago. I've dated since, but nothing too serious."

"Oh." Jessica took a bite of her chicken and watched Ben dig into his mahimahi. She wanted to ask about the relationship that had ended. Who was the woman? What was she like? And how could she have been crazy enough to let a man like Ben go?

Instead, she asked about his meal. "How is your fish?"

He looked up and grinned. "Delicious. Would you like to try it?"

"Sure."

He prepared a bite for her, dipping a piece of mahimahi into the sauce and extending the fork across the table. She leaned forward and closed her mouth over the tines, making a sound of pleasure at the delicate flavor of the fish.

"Wow, that's good," she said.

Ben's expression was intent as he reached toward her and captured a drop of sauce from her upper lip. "You missed some," he said, and without stopping to think she licked the lemony goodness from his finger.

Heat swept through her. Back in New York, she would never have done such a thing on a dinner date. It was so forward, so . . .

Sexual.

She looked up and met Ben's eyes. He was staring at her, his expression smoldering. Her heart started to pound.

She looked back down at her plate, cutting a bite of chicken with trembling hands. They focused on eating for the next few minutes, but the electricity between them was like a living thing.

For the first time since they'd arrived in Bermuda, neither one of them ordered dessert.

As they were leaving the restaurant Ben put a hand on her lower back, and the contact sent a flutter of excitement through her whole body. But when she started to head for the outside doors, he steered her across the lobby instead.

"Where are we going?"

"The cocktail lounge."

She shook her head vigorously. "No. I don't want to drink. I know it would probably relax me a little, but I don't want to—to cheat. That probably sounds stupid to you, but—"

"It doesn't sound stupid," Ben said. "It sounds brave."

"Brave?"

He nodded. "You want to make your own choices, without the help of alcohol. And you can. You don't have to drink to be able to know what you want. That's what this is about, right? Figuring out what you want? What you like?"

"Yes."

"Okay, then. We're not going to the lounge to drink. We're going to dance."

"Dance?"

"There's a band playing tonight. I thought that would be a good start for us."

She thought about it. She didn't really want to dance, but she'd told Ben that she trusted him. That she was putting herself in his hands. "Okay."

They could hear the music before they reached the doorway. Jessica wasn't positive, but she thought the song sounded like . . .

"Oh my God. It's a Journey cover band."

"Not only Journey," Ben said with a grin. "The guy at the desk told me they do a wide variety of eighties songs."

She looked up at him skeptically. "And you think this is a good dating move?"

"We're about find out," Ben said as they went through the entrance to the lounge.

CHAPTER TEN

They stood inside the doorway for a moment, taking in the scene. The lounge was full but not crowded. The couples on the dance floor and at the tables and barstools were mostly over forty, and they looked like they were having a good time.

The band was at the far end of the room. They finished "Don't Stop Believing," paused a moment, and then went into a slow song she didn't recognize.

"Come on," Ben said, taking her hand and leading her onto the dance floor.

"I'm feeling déjà vu," she murmured, letting Ben place her right hand on his left shoulder before he took her left hand in his right. "Do you remember our ballroom lessons at Shipley?"

In seventh grade, all the students had been required to take ballroom dance.

Ben pulled her a little closer. "I remember."

The two of them had agreed to be partners through that year of torture. By the end of it, the half hour devoted to learning the waltz and the fox-trot had turned into her favorite part of the day.

"Should we try to do steps or something?"

The question sounded silly as soon as she asked it, but she felt stiff and she couldn't seem to relax.

"We don't have to do anything fancy," Ben said. "This is a slow song, right? All we have to do is sway."

"Sway?"

"Yeah."

He showed her what he meant by moving back and forth to the beat.

"You're right. This is easy."

"I told you so. All you have to do is trust me. Remember?"

"Yes. I do."

He slid an arm around her waist. "Good."

Millimeter by millimeter she felt herself relaxing. Maybe that was because of Ben, who seemed perfectly relaxed himself, as though he were in no hurry at all. Somehow, her stereotype of men had included the idea that when an offer of sex was on the table, their libido would take the wheel—which would mean getting horizontal as soon as possible.

But Ben wasn't trying to rush her into bed. He was enjoying himself in the moment, with her, swaying to the music of a mediocre eighties cover band.

She let her head fall forward, resting her cheek against Ben's broad chest. She could hear his heart beating. As he changed his hold and enveloped her in his strong arms, his heart beat faster.

Hers was beating faster, too. Ben's body was so warm, so big, so strong and male—but there was nothing intimidating in his masculinity, nothing that made her feel helpless or afraid.

She just felt . . . good.

Her arms were around his waist, her head against his chest. She was surrounded by the scent of clean male skin and the warmth of his presence, and for a few minutes that was all she could focus on.

But below the haze of comfort and ease was a lower, deeper thrum. When the band finished one song and began another, Ben introduced a new rhythm to their dancing.

He insinuated one of his legs between hers as they swayed, and after a moment Jessica realized that she was sort of . . . riding his thigh.

She tensed up for just a moment but Ben eased her even closer, splaying one hand against the small of her back and sliding the other up to the nape of her neck.

She let her head fall forward again. The friction between her legs was subtle but constant, and as Ben shifted with the music, twisting his hips and moving her with him, heat bloomed inside her. It started low in her belly and at the tops of her thighs and then spread through her whole body. A kind of tension coiled between her legs—tension that Ben had created in her and that only he could ease.

"Jessica?"

She lifted her head slowly, as though drugged. And she felt drugged, too—drugged on something ancient but new to her, something she'd never really felt before but that she knew was old as the hills.

Ben's eyes were such a rich, warm brown . . . and now they were hot with desire, the same desire she was feeling. As she looked up at him she saw his pupils dilate until his eyes were almost black.

"Jessica?" he asked again.

"Yes?"

"Close your eyes."

She did. Ben's head dipped toward her as she let her own fall back, and when their mouths touched, the relief was so intense she moaned.

He pulled her tight against him, and she realized for the first time that he was hard for her.

They were in the middle of a room full of people and Ben was hard for her.

Maybe she should have been mortified, but all she felt was excitement. Ben urged her lips apart and she complied eagerly, longing for the invasion of his tongue.

His hands slid into her hair and she shivered all over. She looped her arms around his neck, tugging him down toward her, and relishing the way her breasts flattened against his chest.

She dragged her mouth from his, panting. "Let's go back to the cottage," she said.

He was breathing hard, too. "You sure?"

"Yes. Yes. Yes."

That made him smile, and he grabbed her hand as he pulled her off the dance floor. "Okay, then," he said. "Never let it be said that I can't take a subtle hint."

They stumbled out of the lounge and into the lobby, where he tugged her into a dark corner and pressed her up against the wall.

"Tell me you want me."

His voice was low and rough and so, so sexy.

"I want you," she said, her own voice trembling. "Oh God, I want you so much."

Her reward was another searing kiss, and then Ben grabbed her hand again and pulled her across the lobby to the doors.

Outside a cool breeze was blowing, but her cheeks—her whole body—felt blazing hot.

Suddenly she stopped.

"What is it?" Ben asked, turning toward her.

"Tell me you want me," she said, echoing his words.

He gave a sharp tug on her wrist and then she was in his arms, pressed against him collarbones to thighs.

"I want you," he said, gazing down at her. "I want you more than I've ever wanted a woman in my life. I've wanted you since I was too young to know what that meant. You were my first fantasy, Jess."

Her heart was pounding. "I was?"

"Yeah. The first time I made myself come, you were right there with me."

Her cheeks flamed, and she pressed her forehead to his chest. "Oh my God. Are you serious?"

"Yeah." He slid a hand under her chin and urged her face up again, looking deep into her eyes. "You were the prettiest, sexiest girl I'd ever met, and you still are. So yeah, I want you."

He took her hand and led her down the flagstone path toward their cottage, and even though she hadn't had a drop of alcohol all day, she felt drunk.

This was happening. This was really happening.

They pulled out their key cards at the same time, and they both dropped them. Jessica started to laugh, feeling so good she was almost effervescent. Ben scooped up the cards and waved them in front of the reader.

And then, finally, they were inside.

Ben swept her into his arms and carried her to the bed, laying her down on top of the covers.

"Hey," she said, feeling suddenly shy as she looked up into his face.

"Hey," he answered, supporting his weight on his arms as he looked down at her.

They stayed like that for a moment, desire crackling between them.

"Will you let me make love to you?"

She swallowed. "That's what tonight is about. That's what I want."

He shook his head. "Tonight is about finding out what you like. But we've got a week left on this island, and I want to take full advantage of it. Tonight's just act one."

"What happens in act one?"

"You lie back and I make you come."

Her heart slammed against her ribs. That was probably the sexiest sentence she'd ever heard, but—

"Ben."

"Yeah?"

"You should know that I don't usually . . . that is, I've never come with someone before. I've faked it, but . . . I don't want to do that with you."

He lay down next to her and brushed her hair away from her face.

"Good," he said. "I don't want you to do that, either." He paused. "Have you ever made yourself come?"

Talk about being direct.

Her cheeks flamed. "Yes," she said.

"Good." He leaned over and gave her a quick, hard kiss. "You only have one job tonight. If you don't like something I'm doing, you let me know. And if you like something, you can let me know that, too."

"Okay." She paused. "What should I do first?"

He shook his head. "You weren't listening, were you? I'm doing all the work. And the first thing I'm going to do is take off your clothes."

She was trembling, but she managed to nod. Her blood was leaping with excitement, her heart hammering against her chest, but Ben seemed to be in no hurry.

He moved down the bed and slipped her sandals off first. Then he sat up and pulled her feet into his lap, running his thumbs over her arches until she made a soft sound of pleasure.

"I like that," she said breathlessly.

He smiled at her. "Good. That's what I'm going for. As far as telling me what you like, though—I have an addendum. If you don't feel like talking, please know that I'll accept a moan or gasp in lieu of words."

He slid his hands up her legs and grasped the waistband of her pants, pulling them down and off.

Her breath caught in her chest and she was very glad she didn't need to talk. She was also glad she was wearing pretty underwear. They were lavender satin and—

And Ben was about to get a look at the matching bra.

He was unbuttoning her blouse now, slowly, from the bottom to the top. When it was undone, it fell open, but before she had time to think about him looking at her bra, he slid a hand under her back and unhooked it. Then he was pulling her blouse and bra off together and tossing them aside, and before she knew what was happening, she was half-naked and he was looking at her breasts.

Her heart was pounding. Goose bumps prickled her skin and her nipples hardened, and Ben was seeing it happen.

Raw hunger and reverence came into his eyes. No man had ever looked at her like that, as though he wanted to worship her and devour her at the same time.

Then he lowered his head and covered one breast with his mouth and the other with his hand.

Her hands fisted in the sheets. There was too much sensation to process—his warm, wet mouth and the drag of his teeth and the rough way he handled her, pinching and rolling her nipple in his fingers and then squeezing and biting at the same time . . . too hard and yet not hard enough.

It's too much, she wanted to say.

But instead she arched her back to bring herself closer to him.

A current of electricity sparked from her breasts to the place that throbbed between her legs. And then, before she quite realized what was happening, Ben was kissing his way along that pathway of heat until he reached her panties.

Her legs had fallen open and his big body lay between them. His hands were splayed over her hips and his mouth—

Her muscles tensed and she rose up on her elbows. "Ben?"

He stopped immediately, looking up to meet her eyes. "You okay?"

She swallowed. "I don't know. I mean . . . I feel . . . nervous."

He moved back up the bed until he was lying next to her. "All right," he said softly. "What are you nervous about?"

He reached out a hand to caress her hair, her face, her bare shoulder, and under his gentle touch she felt herself relaxing.

"I don't know if I'm ready to be that, um, exposed." She paused. "I'm sorry for ruining the mood."

For a moment he just looked at her, his dark brown eyes full of heat and affection and lust and tenderness and a hundred other things she couldn't identify. Then he slid both hands into her hair and pulled her against him for a hot, wet, open-mouthed kiss that left her quivering.

"How's the mood now?" he asked. His voice was low and rich and husky, and it played along nerve endings she hadn't known she possessed.

"Pretty good, actually," she managed to say.

He propped himself up on one elbow and looked down at her. "I don't know if this will help, but I feel exposed, too."

She stared at him. "You haven't even taken off your clothes. How can you possibly feel exposed?"

"Because I want you so much."

He rolled onto his back, and for the first time she saw the bulge straining against his pants. "If you want to even out the playing field in terms of clothes, I'm at your mercy." His eyes glittered as he looked at her. "Just promise me you'll be gentle."

She rose up to a sitting position, looking down at him.

Anticipation tingled in her fingertips. Was this really going to happen? Was she really going to undress Ben Taggart?

Yes.

She started with his button-down shirt, taking her time and feeling a rush of excitement when it fell open. His breathing was ragged, his smooth, hard chest rising and falling with his breath, and when she leaned over to press a kiss against his breastbone, he groaned softly.

She kissed her way down his body as he'd done with her, and when she reached the waistband of his pants, she undid his button and his zipper and then pulled them off, letting them fall to the floor.

The only thing between them now was his boxers.

She wanted to touch the hard ridge of his erection. She reached out tentatively and then pulled her hand back, looking up and meeting his eyes.

"What do you want to do?" he asked.

"I want to touch you," she whispered. "Is that . . . do you want that, too?"

He closed his eyes briefly. "I want it so much I'm willing to beg."

A flush of heat warmed her bare skin. "You don't have to beg," she said, leaning forward and putting her hand on the bulge beneath his underwear.

Ben made a low, desperate sound, and that made her feel bolder. She ran her hand up and down his hard length, feeling how much that excited him, and then she squeezed.

"*Jessica.*"

She loved the way he said her name—like a plea or a prayer. She took hold of his boxers and pulled them off, and then, in the grip of fevered desire, she knelt over Ben and took him into her mouth.

He shuddered from head to toe. "Jessica. *Jessica.*"

She couldn't get enough of the way his voice seemed to caress her name, or the taste of his hot, hard length against her tongue, or the feel of his hands in her hair.

She'd never been a big fan of oral sex—giving or receiving—but this was different. This was Ben she was touching, Ben she was tasting, Ben she was driving crazy.

If it had been up to her, she wouldn't have stopped until he exploded. She would have experimented with her hands, her mouth, her tongue, until she found out exactly what would make that happen. But before things could get there, Ben pulled away from her, panting.

"Why did you stop me?"

He surged up to a sitting position, pulling off his shirt and tossing it to the floor.

"Because I don't want to come in your mouth. Not when I could come inside you—if you'll let me."

His words sent an erotic thrill down her spine. "I want both," she said, amazed to hear herself say such a thing.

His eyebrows shot up. "Are you trying to kill me?"

She shook her head. "I just want to experience everything." She hesitated. "With you."

Up until that point, his expression had been all lust with a sprinkling of humor. But now something different came into his eyes—something deeper.

She was kneeling on the bed while he was sitting back against the headboard. Now he reached out and pulled her into his arms, rolling them over until she was on her back and he was above her, his weight supported on his arms and one powerful thigh between her legs.

"You will," he said, his voice husky. "You'll experience everything you want to, Jess. I swear it."

Her eyes fluttered closed. Her naked breasts were pressed against his chest, and the weight of that contact made her heart thud against her ribcage.

But even more urgent was the sensation between her legs.

She didn't realize that she'd started to move against him, twisting and writhing to increase the delicious friction, until Ben started to move, too, his hips flexing and his thigh pushing against her center.

"Oh God," she gasped. "Ben . . . please . . ."

"What?" he murmured in her ear, just before nipping at the tender lobe. "What do you want, Jess?"

"I want you inside me."

He rocked against her and she gasped again. "I want you inside me *right now*."

He kissed her hard and then rolled away to the edge of the bed, opening the drawer of his nightstand and pulling out a pack of condoms.

She rose up on her elbows, staring. "Where did those come from? Please tell me you didn't bring them from New York."

He grinned as he opened the box, and she took a moment to admire his smooth bare skin and the play of hard muscle beneath it.

"I'm not that arrogant," he said. "I bought them our second day here, after we kissed that first night."

"I see. And you didn't think that was arrogant?"

He shook his head. "It was hopeful. I knew you were hot for me, and I was just waiting for you to realize it when you were sober."

He took out a foil packet and started to open it.

"Wait," she said, surprising both of them.

"Do you want to slow down? I'd be happy to go back to the foreplay part of the evening," he added with a wicked grin. "Hell, I get turned on just by kissing you. If you want to spend the whole night necking, I'd be down with that. Whatever you want, Jess."

Her gaze drifted down to his lap. He was hard as granite, long and thick and proudly erect, and yet she knew that if she called a halt, he'd accept it.

A rush of affection went through her, and it made her desire burn even hotter.

"It's not that. I want—I want—" She paused.

Could she really ask for what she wanted? She'd never expressed a desire of her own in bed before. But Ben had made tonight safe and hot and playful and erotic all at the same time, and everything seemed possible with him.

"I want to be on top. And I want to put the condom on you."

He blinked. "Well," he said after a moment. "Your wish is definitely my command."

He handed her the square packet and settled down on his back, folding his arms behind his head and grinning up at her.

"You're the sexiest human being I've ever seen," she said, letting her eyes rove over his powerful body.

"That's my line," he said. "Speaking of which, you still have an article of clothing to remove."

She kept her eyes on him as she put the condom between her teeth. Then she rose up on her knees, hooked her thumbs in the waistband of her panties, and slid them down her legs. She slipped them off and kicked them aside, and then she crawled over to Ben on her hands and knees, the condom still in her mouth.

Ben stared at her, his eyes wide. "What were you saying before about your problem with sex?"

She ripped open the foil with her teeth as she threw her right leg over Ben, straddling him with a knee on either side of his hips.

"I said I thought you were the one who could help me. I was obviously right."

She started to roll the condom over his erection, but it didn't cooperate.

"Other way," Ben grated out.

"Oh." She turned the condom over and tried again, and this time the slick latex moved smoothly over his hard, hot flesh. "I ruined another moment," she said. "I was going for sex kitten and I totally blew it."

"If you climb on top of me right now, I'll forgive you."

She'd never met a man who could be strong and sexy and adorable all at once.

"Okay," she said. "It's a deal."

As she took him in her hand to guide him inside her, she realized just how hot and wet and ready she was.

And then, slowly, she sank down on top of him.

"Jesus," Ben whispered, his eyes closing and his jaw muscles tensing. "You're so tight."

The sensation of fullness spread from her center through her whole body. It shimmered like light through her veins, as though Ben's very essence was mingling with hers.

She put her hands flat on his chest and leaned over him. His eyes opened and he looked at her, and for one searing moment the world seemed to stop spinning.

Her heart stopped. Her breath stopped. All she knew was the joining of their bodies and the depth of his gaze and a longing that couldn't be satisfied even by achieving its desire.

"Jessica," Ben said, his voice shaking.

She started to move, slowly, her eyes still on his. She was so focused on Ben that she didn't realize what was happening in her body until—

"Oh my God," she gasped. "I think I'm going to come." And in the next instant she knew what would send her over the edge. "I want you to be on top when I do. Will you be on top when I—"

He didn't wait for her to finish. He flipped her onto her back without losing the connection of their bodies and drove into her, hard and then harder, until her orgasm began in her fingers and toes before igniting every nerve ending in a glorious explosion.

An instant later she felt Ben pulse inside her. He thrust deep, calling her name, and his head dropped to her shoulder as he shuddered out his release.

The thunder of their heartbeats eventually slowed. Ben shifted slightly to the side, easing the weight of his body on top of hers, but keeping the contact between them.

The aftermath was so sweet she never wanted it to end. Her body was so sated, so replete, that it was impossible to imagine feeling hunger or thirst or need or pain ever again.

Ben seemed to feel the same. His hands moved over her hair, her skin, as though he couldn't stop touching her.

She never wanted him to stop touching her. She felt warm and safe and treasured and . . .

Sleepy.

She yawned hugely and Ben chuckled, the vibration tickling her cheek where it rested against his chest.

"I thought men were the ones who fell asleep after sex," he said softly.

He was rubbing her back in slow circles. She yawned again and snuggled against him, getting as close as humanly possible.

"That was amazing."

Her eyes fluttered closed. She wanted to stay awake longer, to enjoy this moment, but sleep was overtaking her.

"Yeah, it was. If you don't mind my asking, why in the hell did you think you had a problem with sex? What kind of idiots have you been dating?"

She was starting to drift. As she did, the closeness she felt to Ben drew words out of her she'd never spoken to another human being.

"It wasn't their fault," she murmured. "It was me. When I was eleven, my uncle Jeffrey—"

She stopped. Even half-asleep, warning bells went off in her head, and every instinct she possessed made the words stick in her throat.

Beside her, Ben went absolutely still. "Your uncle Jeffrey what?" he asked after a moment.

She woke up a little bit more. "It's nothing. It was a long time ago. It's not important."

"Jessica." Ben put a little space between them and shifted so they were face-to-face. "What did he do?"

She swallowed. Would it be so terrible to tell him?

Maybe not. Maybe it would be all right for one person to know—one person she trusted as much as she trusted Ben.

"He would stop by the house sometimes when my parents weren't home. He'd send the nanny out with Vicki and then, when we were alone . . . he would touch me."

Ben closed his eyes for a moment. When he opened them again, he said, "Your uncle . . ." He stopped and started again. "Your uncle molested you?"

She recoiled at that word—at the ugliness, the darkness, the shame coiled inside it.

"No! He wasn't violent. He didn't . . . he didn't hurt me. It was only touching."

A spasm tightened the muscles of his face. When he spoke again, his voice was low. "I don't think I ever met this guy. Jeffrey, you said? Where is he now?"

Something in his tone raised the hair on the back her neck. "He died of a heart attack a few years ago."

Ben was quiet for a moment. "Do your parents know what he did?"

"No," she said. "Nobody does." She paused. "It didn't happen very often. It ended when I was thirteen, after he moved overseas. It's not a big deal. I mean . . . it was so long ago. I'm not traumatized or anything like that. It didn't affect my life at all, except—" She looked down for a moment. "Except that sex has been hard for me." She looked back at Ben. "That's why I'm so glad that you—that you and I—" She swallowed. "That tonight happened."

Ben slid his hands into her hair, brushing his thumbs over her cheekbones. His eyes roved over her face with an intensity that made her catch her breath.

"So am I," he said huskily. "That was the best sex of my life, Jess."

Her heart soared at those words. Unless . . .

"You're not just saying that because of what I told you? Because you think I'm damaged or something?"

He shook his head slowly, his eyes bright. "I don't think you're damaged. I think you're incredible. I think you're brave, and beautiful, and so damn sexy I want to make love with you all over again."

Relief flooded through her. Telling Ben her secret hadn't changed the way he saw her. "I think I need to rest a little before we do that again. Is tomorrow soon enough?"

"Yeah," he said. "Tomorrow will be good." His hands moved to her shoulders, and he pulled her close. "How's this for good news? We have a whole week to look forward to."

She slid her arms around his waist and nestled against him. "That sounds promising," she murmured.

"Yeah, it does." He held her tighter. "Go to sleep, sweetheart."

Sweetheart.

Her eyes were closing again. "Good night, Ben."

"Good night."

CHAPTER ELEVEN

Jessica looked like an angel with her fair hair scattered over the white pillow. Her eyes were closed; her breathing was slow and even.

Once he was sure she was deeply asleep, Ben slipped noiselessly out of bed, went into the bathroom, and closed the door behind him.

He turned on the shower with shaking hands. He stepped under the spray, braced his arms against the tile, and bowed his head beneath the water.

The intensity of his emotions threatened to rip him apart from the inside.

He'd just had one of the most passionate sexual encounters of his life. His need to give pleasure to Jessica had been like a fire burning in his blood, and only his greater need to make sure he didn't come on too strong had kept his primitive side in check.

Then Jessica told him her secret, and another instinct had taken over.

The urge to hurt someone for hurting her.

It was a good thing the man who'd done that to her was already dead, because otherwise he might have done the job himself.

But there were other people to blame. Her parents, for not protecting her . . . and for not being the kind of people that Jessica could confide in.

And her friends, including himself, for not figuring out that something was wrong.

He thought about her weight gain in junior high and the self-hatred she'd so often expressed. Then he thought about her subsequent weight loss and her rejection of her past self.

A lot of that, if not all of it, must be related to the sexual abuse she'd survived. But it had never occurred to him that she might be dealing with a traumatic event. He'd been just like everyone else in her life—unwilling to look beneath the surface of her behavior to what might have caused it.

This wasn't the first time someone had confided a history of abuse to him. Students would sometimes trust a teacher when they couldn't trust anyone else, and that meant he'd heard some horror stories. He'd done his best to help, taking action when he could and providing support and a safe space when he couldn't.

A string of phrases ran through his mind. Remember that it's about the survivor, not you. The focus can't be on what you feel. If you show shock or devastation at what someone has gone through, you risk adding to their shame and guilt. For their sake, you have to stay strong.

And most difficult of all: remember that this isn't your problem to solve.

Never had all that advice seemed so impossible to follow. Never had he so desperately wanted to fix something he couldn't fix—something Jessica hadn't asked him to fix.

Something she didn't think needed to be fixed.

The shower wasn't helping. An inferno of rage still burned inside his heart, and there was no outlet for it.

Just like Jessica had had no outlet for her fear and confusion and pain all those years when he could have—should have—been there for her.

But blaming himself wouldn't do any good, either. He needed to put his own feelings aside and focus on Jessica.

She didn't want him trying to fix her or heal her. She'd only asked for one thing, and by God, he was going to make sure she got it.

The best sexual experiences he could give her.

~

He woke up when Jessica stirred in his arms. For a moment he held her tighter, as though someone were trying to snatch her away from him. Then he woke up fully, realized what he was doing, and let her go.

She rolled onto her back and smiled at him.

"Hi," she said, her voice a little shy.

He reached out and brushed the backs of his fingers across her cheek. Her skin, warm and rosy with sleep, felt softer than silk.

"Hi," he said.

The covers had slid down to her waist, and he enjoyed the luxury of gazing at her naked body in the light of day. Not satisfied with looking, he trailed his hand down over her collarbones and onto her breasts, relishing her sudden intake of breath and the way her nipples puckered and tightened.

She gazed at him for a moment, her eyes wide and dark and her lips parted. Then she looped an arm around his neck and brought him to her for a kiss.

At the feel of her soft mouth and sweet body, he hardened in a swift erotic rush. He rolled her onto her back and broke the kiss, dragging his mouth down her neck and between her breasts and onto her flat stomach.

Her muscles tightened and her hands slid into his hair.

"Ben!"

He looked up and grinned at her. "Yeah?"

Her golden hair was scattered over the pillow and her face was flushed pink.

"I don't know . . . I'm not sure . . ."

"I want to taste you, Jess. I want to feel you come apart under my mouth. Do you want that, too?"

Her eyes widened and her flush deepened. "Ben," she whispered.

"Is that a yes?"

When she didn't answer, he shifted his weight and settled between her legs, his hands on her hips.

"I'll beg if I have to, sweetheart. Because I've never wanted anything like I want this."

Her lips parted but no sound came out.

"Tell you what," he said softly. "If it's a yes, just nod. You don't have to say a word."

For a minute she just looked at him, and he could see her anxiety warring with her desire.

Then, slowly, she nodded her head.

That was all he needed. He pulled the covers away from her lower body and feasted on the sight of her naked before him, soft and strong and nervous and excited and so goddamn tempting he didn't know how he could rein himself in enough to take this slow.

But he would find a way. Because after last night, he knew that giving Jessica pleasure was the most powerful aphrodisiac he could ever experience.

He put his hands on the insides of her thighs and pushed them wider, making room for himself between her legs. As he gazed down at the soft, delicate folds of her center, he felt Jessica's anticipation as intensely as he felt his own.

Then he lowered his head.

He tasted sex and sweetness and the tang of desire, and as his tongue teased out all her secrets, finding the places that made her writhe and moan, his heart was pounding so hard it made him shake.

When she arched her back with a sudden gasp, he drove her higher, using his thumbs to spread her wide as he flicked his tongue against her throbbing flesh again and again until—

She cried out his name as she came apart, pulsing and throbbing against his mouth until he thought his own body would explode.

He touched her more softly as she came spiraling down. He licked and kissed his way back up her body, relishing every gasp and quiver and quake, until he lay at her side brushing her hair away from her flushed face.

"Oh my God," she said, staring up at the ceiling. "I mean . . . oh my *God*."

He grinned. "So that was okay for you, huh?"

She rolled onto her side to face him. "That was incredible. Do other women know about this?"

A rush of affection mingled with the lust that still heated his body. "This is definitely something that women tend to enjoy, but it's not always like that."

She tucked her arm under her head. "Why not?"

"I have no idea. It's a mystery." He paused. "All I know is that it takes guts to make yourself vulnerable like that. To let someone touch that part of you. I couldn't make you feel good if you didn't let me, Jess. If you didn't trust me."

"I do trust you," she said softly.

For a moment she just looked at him, her eyes delving into his, and he wondered what she was thinking. Then she reached out a hand and ran her fingers along his jaw.

"You're all stubbly," she said.

"Yeah?"

She nodded. "I like it. It suits you."

He grinned at her. "I didn't scratch you?"

"Yes, but in a good way. A really, really good way." She started to say something else and then hesitated.

"What is it? What were you about to say?"

She curled her hands under her chin in a way he found completely adorable. "I thought maybe I could experiment a little."

Her gaze strayed down his torso to the waistband of the sweatpants he'd put on after his shower last night.

His body had calmed a little in the last few minutes, but now he felt himself growing hard.

"Experiment how?" he asked, his voice low and gravelly.

"There's something I want to do that I've never done before. I want to make you come with my mouth. If you'll let me."

He closed his eyes for a second and then opened them. "If I'll *let* you? You made me hard as a goddamn rock just by saying that."

She looked delighted. "I did?"

"Yeah."

"So . . . I have your permission to experiment?"

In that moment, he knew he would never meet another woman who could be so sexy and so adorable at the same time.

"I told you last night I'm here for you, Jess. And if that means being your sexual plaything, well, then, I guess I can put up with it."

Her smile widened, and it made him so happy to see her happy that his heart ached a little.

He felt like he would sell his soul to ensure that she could stay that happy for the rest of her life. But it looked like the only price he had to pay right now was his virtue.

She rose up on her knees and tugged the blankets down. Then she put her small hands on the waistband of his sweats and tugged them down, too.

He helped her by lifting his hips. After she'd tossed the sweatpants on the floor she knelt beside him again, looking him over from head to toe.

After a moment her eyes flicked back up to his face. "You have a really good body," she said, and he grinned.

"You think so? Well, thanks. I'm a fan of your body, too."

"We're doing you right now," she reminded him, leaning forward until the waves of her blonde hair brushed against his chest. She put her hands on his shoulders, leaned down farther, and pressed her lips to his breastbone. Then she wriggled farther down the bed, kissing her way to his abdomen.

He groaned.

"Is this okay?" she asked, looking up at him.

"Hell yeah. But sweetheart—"

"Yes?"

Unable to resist touching her, he ran a hand through her hair. "I should probably warn you . . ."

"Yes?"

"I'm about ready to explode. I don't want you to be, uh, surprised."

"I appreciate the heads-up," she said gravely. "That's very considerate of you."

Then she slid down the bed and took him into her mouth.

He swore out loud and closed his eyes. When she wrapped her hand around his base and squeezed, his hands fisted in the sheets.

Women had gone down on him before, and he'd always enjoyed it. But this was different.

This was Jessica. This was Jessica, taking her time with him the way he'd taken his time with her.

Exploring. Experimenting. Making him feel so damn good he—

"Ben?" she asked, and he opened his eyes again. The sight of her looking up at him like that, his cock in her hand and her soft lips just inches from his fevered flesh, almost made him come then and there.

"Yeah?" he managed.

"I want you to tell me what you like."

Anything you do, he started to say—but then he stopped. He could tell from her expression that this was important to her.

"I like when you use your tongue," he said roughly. "And . . . you can grip me harder, if you want."

She nodded. "What else?"

"It feels good when you take me deep. But if you don't like doing that . . ."

She didn't let him finish. She dipped her head and took him in again, and this time the head of his cock touched the back of her throat.

"*Jessica.*"

She was all over him, hands and mouth and tongue. She went harder and faster until the explosion came, almost blinding in its intensity.

He lay gasping, emptied out, covered in a light sheen of sweat and sex.

He was vaguely aware that Jessica was lying beside him again, trailing her hand down his chest.

"I really enjoyed that," she said, sounding both pleased and surprised.

When he had his breathing under control again, he managed to form a sentence.

"It was pretty good for me, too."

He'd never come with so much feverish urgency. He rolled onto his side to face Jessica, cupping her face in his hands.

"Thank you," he said.

"You're welcome."

The absurdity of that polite exchange after what they'd just experienced seemed to hit them at the same time, and they grinned at each other.

Ben pulled her close and stroked her hair, loving the silken texture against his hand and the soft weight of her against his chest. She made a noise of satisfaction, something between a snort and a sigh, and he held her a little tighter as a surge of protectiveness went through him.

He couldn't remember the last time he'd felt this happy.

~

She seemed to be made of light instead of flesh and blood. Joy pulsed inside her, filling her veins with every beat of her heart.

"What do you want to do today?" Ben asked after a moment, his hand moving softly over her hair.

She thought about it for a second. The world seemed infinitely bigger than it had yesterday, and delightful possibilities beckoned her forward.

And then, suddenly, she knew exactly what she wanted to do that day.

"I'm going to take you snorkeling."

"Snorkeling?" Ben looked skeptical. "I don't know. I don't think I can put that breathing thing in my mouth."

"Considering what I just had in *my* mouth, I'm thinking you can handle it."

He started to laugh, his body shaking until she was laughing, too.

"That's the first dirty joke I've ever told," she said.

"We're lying here naked and the whole room smells like sex. Dirty jokes are appropriate."

She pushed herself up to a sitting position and looked out the window. It was another gorgeous day, with a clear blue sky over sparkling water.

"I promise you'll love it," she said with confidence.

"You do, huh?"

She grinned down at him. "I do."

"Okay, fine. Let's go snorkeling."

They changed into their bathing suits and took the path down to the beach. The sky was clear and cloudless, the water turquoise, and Jessica had to resist the urge to skip across the sand.

They waded out into the ocean until they were waist deep.

"Okay, here's our strategy." She pointed toward the left side of the beach, where an outcropping of rocks created a bay. "That's where we're headed. The closer we get to the rocks the more fish we'll see."

"That's where they hang out?"

"According to the guy at the snorkel shop. Are you ready?"

"As I'll ever be. How does this mask work again?"

He looked genuinely apprehensive, and Jessica felt a rush of sympathy.

"It does feel a little awkward at first, and it's weird breathing through the mouthpiece. But that's only while you're standing up. Once you're in the water, you'll forget you even have it on."

"I will? Why?"

"You just have to trust me on this."

He didn't look convinced, but he nodded. "Okay, I'll give it a shot."

"Good." She reached up and helped him slip the mask over his head. "Put the mouthpiece in and hold it with your teeth. Your face will be in the water, but the tube will be in the air. Got it?"

He nodded and put the tube in his mouth. After a few seconds he spit it out again.

"I don't think I—"

"Let me go first," she said. "Then put your mouthpiece in and lay yourself out on the water right next to me. All right?"

He sighed. "All right."

Jessica pulled on her mask and closed her mouth over the breathing tube. Then she stretched out on the water, bobbing gently on the rolling waves, and waited for Ben to join her.

After a minute he did. When she saw him floating beside her, she reached for his hand, and once she was sure he was all right, she used her feet and her other hand to propel them slowly toward the rocks.

The magic of the ocean world took her as it always did. It was utterly silent but for the sound of her breath, and the water was so clear she could see every grain of sand below her.

Once they reached the rocks, she stopped paddling. She held Ben's hand firmly as they floated side by side, the two of them drifting like seaweed toward the rocks that rose like islands from the ocean floor.

After a minute or two with no fish in sight she wondered if they'd gone somewhere else for the day. And then, like magic, there they were: electric blue and silver gray and neon green, darting here and there singly and in schools, alien creatures in an alien landscape.

It was silent and mysterious and utterly beautiful.

Ben's arm moved into her field of vision, pointing. She turned her head and saw an enormous bright orange fish moving lazily over a patch of coral, its fins as delicate as angel hair.

Ben squeezed her hand in excitement, and Jessica smiled around her mouthpiece. She'd felt the same excitement the first time she'd gone snorkeling. The truth was, she still did.

But she'd never had someone to share it with.

They stayed out for another hour, drifting hand in hand among the rocks and coral and sea creatures. Then Jessica dipped her head a little too deep following a school of fish and got a mouthful of saltwater. She gasped and choked, pulling her gear off and treading water while she got her breath back. Ben removed his own mask and joined her.

"You okay?" he asked.

She nodded. "I swallowed some water, but I'm fine."

She swam closer to him. It was too deep for her to touch bottom, but Ben was able to stand with his head above the water. He was a strong anchor, and she wrapped her legs around his waist as she threw her arms around his neck.

"So what did you think?"

"It was incredible," he said, smiling into her eyes. "It was like being on another planet. Like seeing a dream world that's actually real."

"I know," she said, happiness vibrating through her. "I'm so glad you liked it."

"I loved it," he said. "Thank you for convincing me to do this. You showed me a whole new world today."

She was so used to thinking of Ben as the strong one, the one who had things to teach her. The reminder that she could give him something, too, was as heady as champagne.

"It was my pleasure," she said.

Then she kissed him.

It was like their first kiss that rainy night, except that this time the sun was shining and she was sober and she didn't have to second-guess herself or hold back or wonder if Ben wanted her as much as she wanted him.

The hard-on grinding against her was a pretty good indicator.

It was only when another group of snorkelers floated past that she remembered they were in public . . . and that they didn't have to be.

She tore her mouth from his. "Back to the room?" she asked, panting.

"Hell yes."

～

An hour later they lay curled up together in bed. Ben was spooning her from behind and she was thinking that she never wanted to move again, when her stomach growled.

Ben chuckled. "Hungry?"

She glanced at the clock on the bedside table. "Oh my God. How did it get to be so late? It's lunchtime, and we haven't even had breakfast yet. How did that happen?"

He nuzzled the back of her neck. "Do you need a reminder of how we spent the morning? Because I'd be happy to give you the play-by-play. I'd be even happier to reenact it."

She turned in his arms to face him. "Would it be too decadent to order room service? I'm starving, but I don't want to get up. Ever."

Ben hadn't shaved yet, and the scruff of his beard made him look more rakish than usual. Between the look of satisfaction in his dark eyes and the lazy half smile on his face, he was the embodiment of male contentment.

"I think that's the best idea I've ever heard. Let's do it."

They ended up ordering pizza and eating in bed, which made her feel even more decadent.

"I have to take a shower," she said afterward, dabbing at a drop of tomato sauce on her arm. "I'm disgusting. I'm covered in dried ocean water and pizza and—"

Ben leaned over and kissed her, wet and sloppy and carnal.

"Whatever you're covered in, I like it," he murmured afterward.

She blinked, lost in an erotic haze. "I can't have sex again. Not right now. I just ate, for one thing. And I really do want to take a shower."

He leaned back against the pillows and grinned at her. "That's mighty presumptuous of you, ma'am. Who said anything about sex?"

She gestured toward him. "Everything about you says sex. You're sex incarnate."

His eyebrows shot up. "Sex incarnate? Wow. Nobody's ever called me that before."

"Well, now they have," she said, forcing herself to get out of bed. "I'll see you in a few minutes."

But she saw him sooner than that. She'd only been standing under the spray a few moments when the bathroom door opened, and Ben stood there in all his naked glory.

"I'm covered in ocean water and pizza too. Would you mind if I joined you?"

She'd never showered with anyone before. The idea had never appealed to her . . . until now.

"Okay," she said.

She'd never realized that an activity could be practical and sexy at the same time. Ben washed every inch of her, making her moan when he slipped the washcloth between her legs. Then he let her return the favor, and she appreciated the perfection of his body anew as she scrubbed his smooth skin and felt the bunch and release of his muscles under her hands.

When they were both thoroughly clean, a crazy impulse made her drop to her knees, and Ben groaned when she took him into her mouth. His arm shot out as he braced himself against the shower wall, and she did all the things she knew he liked.

He didn't let her go all the way this time. He pulled her upright before he came, kissing her under the shower spray before turning off the water.

"I honestly didn't come in here for sex," he said, stepping onto the bath mat and helping her out of the shower. "But now that you've gone and done that, I have to have you. Let's get back into bed."

A wild idea came into her head. "There's something I want," she blurted as he was toweling her dry.

He stopped what he was doing. "Anything," he said. "I mean literally anything. You name it and I'll do it."

She turned away from him to face the counter and the mirror behind it.

"I want you to take me from behind," she said quickly, before she could lose her nerve. "Right here, so I can see you."

His eyes met hers in the mirror. "Jesus," he said.

Self-doubt filled her. "Is that too weird?"

He came up behind her and put his hands on her bare shoulders, kissing the crook of her neck.

"Hell no. It's just that you keep surprising me." He paused. "In a really good way."

He straightened up and looked at her in the mirror again. "Wait here and don't move. I'm going to get a condom."

A minute later she was bent at the waist, her hands splayed out on the counter, and Ben was positioning himself behind her. He entered her with one smooth stroke and she moaned, shaken to her core at the feel of his hard length inside her and the sight of him in the mirror, his eyes hooded and his face taut with pleasure.

She stared at him, enthralled. She'd never seen anything so sexy. Ben was all need and passion and raw masculinity, driving into her with one hand on her back and one hand on her hip. It felt so good, so incredible, and yet—

"I don't think I can come like this," she gasped out. "Maybe we should—"

His eyes met hers in the mirror, and a pulse of desire rippled through her.

"You want to come, Jess?"

She nodded, her heart thudding.

"I'm on it."

The hand on her hip slid down between her thighs, and the pad of his middle finger found the place that ached for his touch.

"Oh God."

Every time Ben thrust inside her she bumped against his hand, and as he started rubbing in hard, tight circles, her bones and muscles seemed to dissolve in pleasure, waves and ripples and arrows of pleasure that rose into a wild crescendo.

Chapter Twelve

S hould we order room service for dinner?" Ben asked.
He was hoping the answer would be yes.

They'd spent the afternoon cuddled up in bed, reading and talking and—incredibly—making love again. Afterward they'd fallen asleep in each other's arms, waking up an hour later to find that it was almost dinnertime.

"I've never spent a day like this in my life," Jessica murmured.

She was lying naked in the circle of his arms. She seemed to glow with vitality and contentment, and he pressed a kiss to the top of her head.

"It suits you," he said, and she tilted her head back to look at him.

"You're just saying that because you're getting laid every few hours."

He grinned down at her. "Very possible. But I notice that you're not complaining."

She shook her head slowly. "Nope. No complaints here." She stretched, the movement making her look as lazy and graceful and sinuous as a cat, and then she rose to a sitting position. "But we can't order room service again. Can we?"

"Who's going to stop us?"

She blinked. "You know, you're right." She sat up straighter. "Let's do it," she said decisively. "Let's order room service for dinner."

"That's the spirit. I'll get the menu."

He ordered a cheeseburger and fries while Jessica decided on a salad. A little while later they were digging into their food out on the patio as the sun sank into a bed of glory.

He was thinking about other blissful moments in his life, wondering if any of them could compare with this one, when Jessica's phone vibrated.

She glanced at the screen and frowned. She hesitated a moment, her brow furrowed and her teeth sunk into her lower lip, before accepting the call.

"Hi, Tom."

Her ex-fiancé was calling her?

Jessica rose to her feet and wandered a short distance away, listening as the other man spoke. Ben grabbed his beer and went inside, wanting to give her privacy.

A few minutes later she popped her head in. "You should come back out if you don't want me to finish your fries," she said.

He joined her at the table again. "Everything okay?"

"Yes." She took a sip of water and leaned back in her chair, gazing out at the sunset over the ocean. "He wanted to be sure I was all right. He feels pretty guilty about everything."

"Yeah, well, he's got reason to feel guilty."

Jessica shook her head. "I don't blame him for anything that happened. We both made choices out of fear, and I'm glad he found the courage to make a better choice before it was too late."

It was a generous thing to say, but . . .

"What about you?" he asked.

She looked at him. "What do you mean?"

"What about your choices? What are you going to do when we get back to New York?"

Her face tensed a little, and he wondered if he should let it go.

"I'm not sure." She hesitated. "Although . . . Tom actually offered me a job. Or, well, conveyed an offer from Everett."

"From Everett?"

She nodded. "He works for the Wildlife Foundation. That's how we met." She smiled faintly. "I introduced him to Tom a few years ago. Now he's moving to New York to head up their office there, and he wants me to do some fund-raising work for them."

Huh. "I don't have particularly friendly feelings for Tom or Everett, but I have to say, that's actually a pretty good idea. Are you going to consider it?"

She shrugged. "I don't know." She paused. "I'm grateful to them for the suggestion, though. And I'm glad that Tom called. I don't want to lose his friendship."

"He should be worried about losing your friendship."

She shook her head. "He won't. There were times in my life when Tom was the only person I could stand to be around. He's got a place in my heart forever."

If Ben hadn't been so proud and so blind years ago, he could have been there for Jessica . . . and then maybe he would have a place in her heart, too.

Guilt was followed by regret. As incredible as their time here was, it couldn't grow into anything else once they left Bermuda. He was leaving for Chicago in two months.

Given that reality, he supposed he should be glad that she had Tom in her life.

"Does Tom know what happened with your uncle?" he asked.

Jessica looked startled and wary. "No, of course not."

"Why of course not?"

"Because nobody knows. It's not something I talk about." She paused. "I don't want to talk about it now."

He'd decided last night that he would follow Jessica's lead. Things might be different if he were staying in New York—if he could be a permanent part of her life going forward. But since he couldn't, what right did he have to give her advice, or push her to talk about things she wasn't ready to talk about?

No right at all. And so he let it go—for the moment.

But later that night, when he was holding Jessica in his arms and marveling at her beauty and sweetness and the strength she would never give herself credit for, he knew he wouldn't be able to stay silent. For better or worse, he had to tell her what he thought.

His place in her life was a temporary one, and there wasn't much he could give her. Great sex didn't count—that was a gift they'd given each other.

Other than that, there was really only one thing of value he had to offer.

Honesty.

"Jessica."

She stretched luxuriously and smiled up at him. "Yes?"

There was probably a way to approach this subject that wouldn't make Jessica feel defensive. But if he waited until he could figure it out, he would never say anything.

Better to say it bluntly than not to say it at all.

"I think you should see a therapist when you get back to New York."

She froze, just as he'd feared she would. "I said I don't want to talk about that."

She was lying on her back and he was on his side, facing her. He reached out, very gently, and brushed a strand of hair away from her face.

"I don't want to talk about it, either," he said. "I don't want to do anything that makes you sad or angry or uncomfortable. If you want the truth, all I want to do is kiss every inch of your body from now until we have to leave this island."

Her face softened a little. "That sounds good to me." She paused. "I told you before, Ben—you don't have to fix me." She reached out a hand and caressed the side of his face. "Well, except for that one thing. And, you know, mission seriously accomplished."

By which she meant sex.

He was glad they'd been able to go there together. He'd never been happier to help a friend with a problem.

But as he phrased it that way to himself, he remembered something she'd said last night.

I thought maybe it's not too late. To have a normal sex life. When I get back to New York . . .

When she got back to New York.

She'd wanted his help so she could have a healthy, sexually fulfilling relationship . . . with someone who wasn't him.

As soon as he thought that, he realized how much he hated the idea of Jessica moving on from him to some other guy. How much he hated imagining her sharing herself with someone else the way she'd shared herself with him.

It made him jealous as hell.

And that realization, as much as anything else, strengthened his determination to tell Jessica the truth. Because if he was feeling jealous of guys Jessica hadn't even met yet, then he had his own selfish impulses where she was concerned—including the impulse to let things ride, to lose himself in the incredible sexual haze they'd created and leave her to face difficult realities some other time . . . if she ever did.

Jessica had enough people in her life who put their own needs before hers. He wasn't going to be one of them—even if he paid a price for honesty.

He leaned over and kissed her. "But the fact that I don't want to talk about it doesn't mean I won't. Because I care about you. And I think you need to find a therapist you can trust. Someone who can help you work through some things."

She moved away from him a little, shifting onto her side and pulling the blankets up to her chin. It was a defensive posture, but she hadn't left the bed yet, and he took that as a good sign.

"I don't need help. I don't want to talk about this."

He was quiet for a moment. "Why not?"

Her eyes searched his. "Because I've spent years learning how not to think about it. Because it's ugly. Because it's dark and twisted and shameful."

He wanted to reach out and pull her into his arms. Instead he said, "What your uncle did was shameful. But there's no reason for you to feel ashamed. There's nothing ugly or dark or twisted about you, Jess."

She took in a deep breath and let it out slowly. "You don't understand."

"Then help me understand."

Her expression was half angry, half miserable. "He used to come into my bedroom. You remember all those posters I had?" She swallowed. "I used to lie there in my bed while he touched me. I thought if I looked hard enough at the animals on my walls that they would save me, somehow. In the beginning I used to fantasize that they would come to life and attack him." She paused. "When I got older, though, I stopped imagining that. I stopped thinking at all. I just stared at those posters and wished I could disappear."

It took every ounce of his strength to rein in the feelings of rage and helplessness at what she had gone through. The feelings of guilt because he hadn't known. Hadn't protected her. Hadn't saved her.

But his own feelings didn't matter. Only Jessica mattered. And if she was strong enough now to lance some of this poison, he was strong enough to listen.

"When I was thirteen, his company transferred him to China. The day he left, I tore down all those posters I'd loved so much. I threw away my dolphin necklace because I'd worn it some of the times he was with me. I got rid of everything I'd loved, because he'd ruined all of it. He'd taken everything I had, everything that felt like a part of me, and twisted it into ugliness. So I decided that I wouldn't love anything anymore. I decided I'd rather be empty than full of things that meant something to me, things someone else could corrupt and destroy. I bought new posters for my walls. Posters of bands I didn't know and movies I hadn't seen and things that didn't mean anything to me. I made friends who didn't mean anything to me. I lived a life that didn't mean anything to me."

Tears were slipping down her cheeks, but she didn't bother to wipe them away. "And now that I'm starting to feel like something good might be possible . . . like it might be safe to love something again . . . I'm terrified that he still has the power to destroy it, some-how." She squeezed her eyes shut. "And that's why I don't want to talk about it, or find a therapist, or think about it ever again."

She pressed her lips tight, but she couldn't stop them from trembling. And then, with a wrenching shudder, she began to sob.

Ben pulled her into his arms and held her tight. And as she cried and shook, he willed love into her as though it were something tangible, a weapon he could use to drive out the fear and darkness she'd carried with her for so long—the burden she should never have had to bear.

Eventually her sobs slowed. She took a few deep breaths and then pulled away from him, rolling onto her back and staring up at the ceiling.

"I'm sorry," she said, sounding hopeless. "This is what I didn't want to happen. This is why I didn't want to talk about this. Now you'll think—" She stopped.

"Now I'll think what?"

She turned her head to look at him.

"Now you'll think of this when you think of me."

They'd spent most of the last twenty-four hours without a stitch on. But something about her eyes right now made Jessica seem more naked, more raw and vulnerable and exposed, than he'd ever seen her before.

"You're afraid this has poisoned things somehow. You're afraid that what your uncle did to you made you worthless and ugly and unlovable. You're afraid that if someone finds out about it, it will change the way they see you."

She nodded slowly. "Yes," she whispered.

"Well, it has changed the way I see you—but not in the way you think." He sat up to make his point. "I didn't know how strong you were. How brave. I didn't know you were a survivor. And now that I do know, I admire you more than you can imagine."

She stared at him. "But I'm not strong. I'm not brave. I dealt with what happened to me by turning my back on everything I cared about. Everything I used to be." She bit her lip. "I turned my back on you."

"You did what you had to do. And it worked, Jess—because you're still here. So thank God you did what you needed to. I'm grateful for all of it, because you survived. But, sweetheart . . . you don't have to use the same tools you did when you were thirteen. You're a grown woman now, brave and strong and beautiful, and he doesn't have power over you anymore. Talking to people you trust—and to people who are trained to help—won't make you weaker. It will only make you stronger." Unable to stop himself from touching her, he reached out and ran the backs of his fingers over her cheek. "And telling your story won't make anyone love you less. It will only make them love you more."

A flush spread over her face, and he realized belatedly that he'd used the word *love*.

Well, damn. Talk about confusing an issue. Of course he loved Jessica—as a friend—but when you were buck-naked in bed with someone, you risked opening yourself up to misunderstanding when you used that word.

The last thing Jess needed to worry about was the possibility that he was falling in love with her. One of the reasons she'd asked him for help with her "problem" was the fact that he was moving to Chicago.

She didn't want a relationship. She wanted a fling. A friends-with-benefits arrangement that would end when their trip did.

And considering everything that was going on in her life, she'd made the right call. She didn't need emotional complications thrown into the mix. Jessica was rebuilding her life from the ground up. She should make decisions based on what was best for her, without regard to anyone else—and without a man putting romantic pressure on her.

Not that he would do that, of course. He wasn't falling in love with Jessica. He cared about her, he admired her, he loved her as a friend—but that was all.

What happened in Bermuda would stay in Bermuda. That was the agreement they'd made, and he would stick to it.

"I'm sorry for pushing you on the therapy thing," he said, wanting to put the "love" moment behind them and get the focus back where it should be. "I made the suggestion because I believe it can help, and because I thought you might be avoiding it when you don't have to. That's all."

She seemed as ready as he was to move on. "I know," she said. "And I promise I'll consider it. And . . . I appreciate everything you've said." She smiled a little tremulously. "I'm glad you pushed me, Ben. I think maybe I needed to be pushed." She paused. "You're a good man, you know. A really good man."

He was probably overanalyzing, but that sounded like a consolation compliment. "I'm just being a friend."

Her eyes searched his. "A friend," she repeated. "Of course."

There was a short silence—a strangely charged silence. Ben felt something building up in him, and he was half afraid to find out what it was.

He cleared his throat. "How would you feel about a midnight hot fudge sundae? Room service stays open twenty-four hours."

She rose up on her elbows and smiled. "I think that's the best idea I ever heard."

CHAPTER THIRTEEN

The rest of the trip went by much too quickly.

Every morning she woke up in Ben's arms, suffused with warmth and security and tenderness—and a glow that came from incredible sex.

After basking in that glow a little while, the first thing she did was calculate the days they had left.

We still have five days.

We still have four days.

We still have . . .

Until, finally, it was the last morning.

Packing was a wrench, as was leaving the cottage for the last time. In ten days it had come to feel more like a home than any she'd ever known.

It wasn't the space that made a home, she realized. It was what you felt when you were in it.

Returning their rented snorkel gear felt ridiculously sentimental. The two of them had spent hours swimming and snorkeling at different spots around the island.

Their luggage was stacked neatly by the front doors, ready for their departure, when they went into the restaurant for breakfast.

"This is the last egg-white omelet I'll have in Bermuda," she murmured, holding her plate out to the chef at the buffet line.

"What's that?" Ben asked.

She shook her head. "I'm being silly. Ignore me."

They carried their plates to a small table by the window—the table they thought of as "theirs."

Ben stayed standing after he set his plate down. "Will you order coffee for me? There's something I need to pick up."

"Sure."

The omelet was delicious. Jessica gazed out the window as she ate, noticing that it looked like it might rain later in the day.

It was impossible to think of rain without thinking of their first night here.

Not that she'd ever forget it.

Ben came back a few minutes later. He took his seat and handed her a small white box with the hotel's gift shop logo stamped on it.

"Here you go," he said. "I've been waiting for this to come in all week."

He'd gotten her a present?

"But I didn't get you anything."

He smiled. "Buy my breakfast and we'll call it even," he said. "This is a tchotchke. It cost me eighteen bucks."

She lifted the lid from the box and looked inside.

On a nest of white cotton lay a silver necklace with a blue enamel dolphin charm.

Ben reached out and turned it over, and she saw that it was engraved on the back.

JESSICA

"They had every other J name in stock," he said. "Jill, Jane, Judy, you name it. But they were out of Jessicas. They ordered this for me, but I wasn't sure it would get here in time." He paused. "I picked it out after your day with the dolphins. I know the memories of your old necklace are complicated, but this one is for all your new memories."

She took the necklace out and laid it on her hand. It wasn't exactly like the one she'd worn as a girl, but it was similar.

"Hey," Ben said, sounding concerned—which was when she realized she was crying.

"I'm sorry," she said, grabbing her napkin and wiping her eyes. "I love it. It's perfect. I just . . . wasn't expecting a present." She handed him the necklace and turned her head. "Would you put it on me?"

"I'm glad you like it," Ben said as he fastened the clasp. "I thought about looking for something else, but—"

She turned around again and faced him, holding the charm against her heart with one hand. "You couldn't have found anything better than this."

~

A few hours later, they were on the plane heading back to New York.

What if she moved to Chicago?

When the idea had first occurred to her, it had seemed like a crazy fantasy. But every time it came back, she dwelled on it a little longer.

Now she found herself wondering if it could be more than a fantasy.

It wasn't like she had anything waiting for her in New York. Other than the possibility of a job with the Wildlife Foundation—a job she didn't know much about yet—what was she going back to?

The aftermath of her disastrous wedding. Twitter hashtags and other humiliations. An empty apartment and her parents' disappointment.

She hadn't spoken with them since the day of the wedding. There had been some emails and texts back and forth, but the two times they'd called she'd let it go to voice mail.

She'd dreaded listening to the messages, but they weren't as bad as she'd feared. Her mother's voice was stiff but her words were kind, and her father had sounded positively sympathetic. Tom had met with them in person—he'd told her about that himself when he'd called—and she gathered that he'd taken the blame for everything. He'd also offered to repay them for the wedding costs, which had done a lot to earn their forgiveness.

Apparently that forgiveness was also going to extend to her, although they'd made it clear they still disapproved of her and Tom's actions and would expect an apology once she got back to the city.

They'd also broached the idea of her selling the new apartment and moving back in with them. But after ten days in Bermuda with Ben, she knew she could never live with her parents again. Until the day came when she could share her life with someone, she would live alone.

The idea of living alone didn't scare her anymore. Because of the strength Ben had helped her find, she was no longer afraid of who she was.

But of course, it would be even better to live with the man she loved.

Ben had come close to saying the words once, but even though he hadn't voiced the sentiment out loud, she was sure of his feelings. She was sure he loved her.

If only he weren't moving away, their relationship would have a chance to evolve organically. They could date for a while, like a normal couple . . . and then, when she felt ready, she could tell him she loved him.

Those words had always stuck in her throat. Her uncle had told her he loved her—one more way he'd taken something that was supposed to be beautiful and twisted it into something ugly. Her parents had told her they loved her, but their love had always come with expectations. Boyfriends had told her they loved her, but that had never stopped them from leaving.

If Ben told her he loved her, it would be different. If Ben said those words to her, she was sure she could say them back . . . eventually. If she had more time.

But they didn't have time. Ben was moving away. He was going out of her life . . . unless something changed.

And of the two of them, she was the one who could most easily make a change. Her most important possession now was something she carried with her: a new determination to live her life with passion.

A determination that Ben had helped her find.

She was trying to think of a way to broach the subject when Ben gave her an opening.

He glanced up from his smartphone. "Did you know that there are dolphins at the Shedd Aquarium in Chicago?"

She blinked. "What?"

"I just looked it up." He grinned. "So if you ever want to visit me, we'll have something to do."

She took her courage in both hands. "About that . . ."

He was looking at his phone again. "Yeah?"

"I was just thinking. Since I don't really have any set plans . . . or, you know, commitments . . ." She took a breath. "Well, there's no reason I have to figure out my next move in New York. I mean, I could look for a job anywhere. Like . . . say . . . Chicago."

Her heart was beating so hard the rush of blood was like thunder in her ears.

Ben shook his head, his expression reassuring. "I know you're kidding, but you shouldn't worry about going back to New York."

Okay, not the response she'd been hoping for. "But—"

"New York is your town, Jess. I know your last experience there was lousy, but that doesn't mean you need to run away." He smiled. "You don't even have to joke about it."

Ben thought she was joking. That's how ridiculous the idea of her moving to Chicago seemed to him.

She bit her lip. "But you were the one who told me to run away. The night of the reception."

"Sure, for a week or two. But now you're ready for real life again. And you're going to do great."

Real life. As in life without Ben.

He couldn't have made it clearer that what they'd had in Bermuda was over now. A wonderful interlude, but nothing more.

She was in the window seat again, and she was grateful for that now. She looked out at the endless blue sky and took a deep breath, disciplining herself not to show what she was feeling.

After a moment she was able to turn back to Ben with a smile.

"I hope so," she said lightly.

He reached out and took one of her hands in his, and the way her body responded—a rush of heat and longing—was one more thing she had to hide.

"You don't have to hope," he said. "I've never believed in anyone more than I believe in you." He squeezed her hand. "I know you've been making lists in your head. What are you going to do when you get back?"

She hadn't been making lists. She'd been thinking about Ben and imagining a future with him.

But it turned out the only place that future would exist was in her imagination.

She had to get a grip on herself. What *was* she going to do when she got back home? What did she want to do?

She thought about it for a moment. And then she realized that she had an answer to that question.

"I'd like to spend more time with my sister. I'd like to spend more time with my friends, too, especially Kate and Simone. I'd like to talk to Everett about the job Tom mentioned—doing fund-raising for the Wildlife Foundation." She paused. "And I'd like to look into the therapy thing. As a possibility."

"That sounds like a pretty good plan to me," Ben said.

When she looked at her watch, she saw that they were more than halfway to JFK. In less than an hour their trip would be officially over.

Ben threaded his fingers with hers. "I've got to say, though . . . I wish we could have stayed in Bermuda a little longer."

She mustered up a smile. "Me too."

He hesitated. "I swore to myself I wasn't going to ask you this."

Suddenly her heart was pounding again. "Yes?"

"I'll be in New York for the rest of the summer. I'd love to keep seeing you, Jess—if that's something you're interested in."

And just like that, her heart plummeted.

He wanted what they'd had in Bermuda: sex and friendship. He wasn't trying to figure out a way they could have more than that— he wanted to keep doing what they'd been doing.

Well, why not? It was the best time she'd ever had in her life, and it was obvious Ben had had a pretty good time, too. She couldn't blame him for suggesting they continue their arrangement for a few more weeks.

But she knew in her heart that it would be different now. Because now she'd want more. And the knowledge that Ben didn't would cut like a knife.

"I don't think so."

He looked taken aback, and she realized she'd spoken more abruptly than she'd intended to.

"I just think . . . once we get back . . . I should focus on the future."

Ben was silent for a moment. "Yeah," he said. "Of course. That makes sense."

Jessica turned her head to look out the window again.

She was suddenly conscious of the weight of her necklace. She was wearing a V-neck top, and the dolphin charm rested against her bare skin.

How had this happened? When they'd boarded the plane, she'd been as sure of Ben's feelings—and her own—as she'd ever been about anything. And now . . .

She took a deep breath. The reality was, nothing had actually changed. She and Ben had had a wonderful time in Bermuda. He'd given her a priceless gift—not just sexual passion, but the seed of her passion for life. A seed that had been so long buried she'd forgotten it existed.

The fact that she'd nourished a foolish, unrealistic hope that they might have a future together didn't negate everything that had happened between them.

"I'm sorry," she said suddenly, turning to Ben. "I didn't mean to sound like . . ."

He smiled at her. "Like you were rejecting me?"

Well, at least she wasn't the only one who felt that way.

"Right," she said. "Because I'm not. I mean . . . I guess I am, sort of. It's just . . ."

"It's okay," he said. "That's what we agreed to, isn't it? What happens in Bermuda stays in Bermuda."

She nodded. "Right." She paused. "I just want you to know . . ."

He shook his head. "That's okay," he said. "You don't have to do that."

"Do what?"

"Tell me how amazing our trip was. I was there, remember?"

"Yes," she said. "I do."

A little while later, the captain announced that they were beginning their descent toward New York City.

She'd better get ready for hers, too. Because the honeymoon was over, and real life was about to begin.

A real life she was going to embrace—even if Ben couldn't be a part of it.

CHAPTER FOURTEEN

How the hell had he screwed up so badly?

That was the question that haunted Ben over the next few days, as he started to get ready for his move to Chicago.

There was plenty to do. Packing, planning, long-distance apartment hunting . . . and he only had six weeks to do it in. He should have been focused on his extensive task list and on spending time with friends and family before he left New York.

But all he could think about was Jessica.

He'd been so sure she'd want to keep seeing him in the time he had left. How could he have read her so wrong?

It wasn't that he didn't understand her decision. She had a lot going on right now, emotional stuff as well as life stuff. She didn't need to deal with him on top of all that—especially when she'd been so clear that they would only be together while they were in Bermuda.

So yes, he understood her decision. There was a lot going on in his life, too. But the fact was, none of his obligations would have stopped him from seeing Jessica if she wanted to see him.

Maybe that was part of the problem. Maybe he'd come on too strong—especially for a guy who'd be leaving town next month.

He shouldn't have talked about the dolphins at Shedd Aquarium. Maybe that had scared her. But how could he not suggest that she come to visit him, after the intensity and passion they'd shared?

Could she really draw a line under that experience and move on as though nothing was different? Because he couldn't.

No . . . it wasn't talking about the dolphins at Shedd that had done it. Because right after that, Jessica had made a joke about Chicago herself.

I could look for a job anywhere. Like . . . say . . . Chicago.

He'd assumed she was making a joke because she was nervous about going home. Something along the lines of, *New York is the last place I want to be right now. I'm dreading it so much I'd even consider moving to Chicago.*

His response had been to reassure her that she had nothing to worry about. That New York City was her home and she'd do great there.

But it was after that part of their conversation that the dynamic between them had changed.

He was lying awake in bed, something he'd done every night since they got back from Bermuda. Now he clasped his hands behind his head, stared up at the ceiling, and replayed the airplane conversation one more time.

Was it possible that Jessica hadn't been joking? That her remark didn't have anything to do with anxiety about returning home? That she was actually willing to consider moving to another city to be with him?

It seemed insane. Why would Jessica uproot herself and come with him to Chicago? Unless . . .

Unless she'd fallen in love with him the way he'd fallen in love with her.

The way he'd . . .

His thoughts stuttered and stopped.

Time seemed to slow. Everything seemed to slow. In the silence and stillness, every heartbeat seemed to have significance.

He'd fallen in love. He'd fallen in love, dammit, and he'd been too blind to see it.

He took in a deep breath and exhaled slowly.

Okay, so he was in love. But what about Jessica? Was there a chance she felt the same way? If there was—if there was even a shadow of a chance—didn't he owe it to both of them to see if it could lead anywhere?

He sat up in bed, full of determination. He grabbed his phone to call her but balked when he saw how late it was.

Damn.

They hadn't had any contact since saying goodbye at the airport—a few short words and an awkward hug that had been a million miles from the intimacy and passion they'd shared in Bermuda. Home that night in his empty bed, he'd woken up more than once reaching for Jessica . . . only to realize she wasn't there.

Three more nights had gone by since then. He'd finally called her this afternoon, only to get her voice mail.

He should have left a message—something friendly and casual. But when he'd heard her voice, he'd choked.

He'd disconnected the call without saying anything. He'd berated himself for freezing up, but then he remembered that her call history would let her know he'd reached out to her. If she wanted to call him back, she could.

But she hadn't called back. What kind of signal did that send him?

She wasn't missing him the way he was missing her. Her heart wasn't aching the way his was. She didn't feel lost without him the way he felt without her.

Or maybe she did, and she just didn't know how to tell him. Maybe she hadn't called him back because she didn't know what to say.

Of course she might still call. Tomorrow, maybe, or the next day.

Male pride dictated that the next move be hers. Calling her again before she returned his call reeked of desperation. By the time he'd gone to bed that night, he'd decided the only thing he could do was wait.

But that was before the realization that he was in love with her had hit him like an anvil. Male pride be damned—he was going to tell her how he felt.

But he had to do it right, which meant in person. So the first step was to get her to meet him.

It was too late for a phone call. But he could text, right? If she happened to be awake, she could answer. If not, she could answer him tomorrow.

It was a decent plan. But what the hell was he going to say?

After a long moment, inspiration struck. He double-checked a sports news item he'd seen that morning and then tapped out a message.

ICYMI: Bermudian cricket star Charles Tucker hits 11 sixes and 6 boundaries and scores a 37 ball century.

As soon as he hit Send he wished he'd just waited until the morning and called her. Because now he was going to lie awake like a goddamn teenager wondering if she'd seen his text or if she was sleeping or—

His phone vibrated.

Tell the truth. You don't have any idea what that means, do you?

His heart sped up.

Not a clue. Do you want to explain it to me over coffee sometime?

Less than a minute had elapsed between his first text and her response. This time, it was a good three minutes before his phone buzzed again—long enough to complete his transformation from grown man to adolescent boy.

How about next weekend? Say 2pm Saturday at the Central Park Café?

That was a week away. He wanted to see her sooner—right this minute, in fact—but Jessica was worth waiting for.

Sounds great. See you then.

After another hour spent tossing and turning, he finally fell asleep. He dreamed that he met Jessica for coffee like they'd planned . . . but when he tried to speak, only nonsense words came out.

∾

Ben got to the café ten minutes early on Saturday, but Jessica was there before him. It was a sunny day and she was sitting at one of the outdoor tables, sipping an iced tea and reading something on her phone.

It had been ten days since he'd seen her. At his first glimpse of her, an electric surge went through him.

She was wearing khaki slacks and a sleeveless white blouse. Her fine blonde hair was held away from her face with a blue cotton headband. Her face, perfectly made up, looked focused and concentrated on whatever she was reading.

She looked gorgeous, but then she always did. His reaction to her ran much deeper than his body's response to her physical beauty.

He knew the mind and heart and soul behind that beauty. He knew Jessica's strength and vulnerability, her fears and her courage, and the light inside her that had refused to die.

It was that light that drew him to her.

And now, as he shook himself out of his stillness and walked toward her, he knew that it always would.

She looked up when he was a few paces away, and a smile lit up her face.

That smile did something to him. It made him feel ten feet tall, as though there could be no greater accomplishment than being the reason Jessica smiled like that.

"Hey," he said as he took the seat across from her, wincing a little at the inanity of the greeting.

"Hey," she said back, slipping her phone into her pocket.

There was a pause. Ben started to say something innocuous about the weather, but he found himself remembering his dream and the words stuck in his throat.

His mother liked to say he had the gift of gab. Jamal had told him once he could talk anywhere, anytime, about anything. His students just said he talked too much—although they also said he managed to explain formulas and algorithms in a way that didn't make their heads explode.

The upshot was that Ben never had trouble thinking of what to say or how to say it. But right now, staring at Jessica like a man who has seen an oasis after days in the desert, he couldn't seem to form words.

"So," Jessica said after a moment.

Ben just waited, hoping she'd continue and save him from having to speak.

"So," she said again. She folded her hands on the rickety wooden table and leaned forward, reminding him of that night in Bermuda—the night she'd asked for his help.

Just like he had then, he mirrored her posture, folding his hands on the table and leaning toward her. "Are you looking for legal advice?"

She snickered. And just like that, the awkwardness between them was gone.

"I'm glad you suggested this," she said, relaxing back in her seat and smiling at him.

He smiled back, and it occurred to him that nothing in his life had ever come easier than smiling at Jessica. "Yeah?"

She nodded. "There's something I want to tell you."

His heart beat a little faster. "There is?"

"I had an appointment yesterday. With a therapist."

Other than a declaration of love, it was the best news he could have heard. "That's great, Jess. How was it?"

"It was good." She paused. "Well . . . not exactly good. Not yet. It was more like I could see that it would be good, someday—after a lot of work. Does that make sense?"

"It makes a lot of sense. You liked this therapist, then?"

"I did. A friend recommended her, and even though I've only seen her once, I can tell she's good at her job. I think I'll be able to trust her . . . eventually. With time." She took a breath. "I'm going to be seeing her two or three times a week at first, which will be intense. But I think I can do it."

He reached out and covered her hands with his. "I know you can. You're one of the strongest people I've ever known, Jess."

It had been an automatic gesture, an instinctive urge to comfort. But at the feel of her small hands in his, her soft skin against his callused palms, his heart started to pound.

Jessica's cheeks turned pink. "Thank you." She pulled her hands away and sat back in her chair again, and he did his best to pretend he didn't miss the contact.

"That's not all that happened this week," she went on. "I also met with Everett."

"Tom's boyfriend?"

She nodded, and suddenly she was grinning. "There's a new Wildlife Foundation initiative dealing with climate change and marine life, and Everett asked me to head up their fund-raising arm. I'll be starting next week. Oh, Ben—fund-raising is work I understand, work I'm actually good at . . . and I'd be doing it for a company I've always loved. What do you think of that?"

"I think it's amazing. Tell me more."

"It's going to be crazy busy until we get some systems in place and do some hiring, but I don't mind. I want to be busy. I want to work hard. I wake up in the middle of the night thinking about all the things I want to do, and I keep a notebook by my bed so I can write down my ideas. I've never been so excited about a job. Everett introduced me to some of the people I'll be working with, and they're incredible. I think I want to—"

As Jessica kept talking, Ben felt like two different people.

One of them was proud of his old friend. She sounded so good—so excited for the future, so full of life. This was what he wanted for her. This was the Jessica he'd always known she could become.

But the other part of him felt his heart sinking to his toes. There was no way he could derail what was happening in Jessica's life. No way he could ask her to come with him to Chicago—not now.

So as he listened to Jessica talk about making her dreams come true, he allowed his own dream to die. Because in the end, what he cared about was Jessica's happiness.

Ever since the night he'd texted her, the night he'd realized he loved her, he'd been thinking about how to tell her. Imagining himself saying the words.

It had never occurred to him that he might decide not to tell her. But hearing her now, seeing her now, he knew those words would have to go unsaid. Because telling Jessica he loved her would only complicate her life, and not in a good way.

They were in completely different places. They weren't focused on the same things. When he woke up in the middle of the night, he thought about Jessica. When she woke up in the middle of the night, she thought about her new job.

When she'd said that, he'd remembered himself as a young teacher. Fresh out of school, he'd been so full of energy and enthusiasm that he'd wake up at two in the morning with his mind full of lesson plans. Romantic love was the last thing he'd thought about in those days.

That's where Jessica was. All her passion and excitement was being poured into her new job, and any emotional energy she had left over would be directed toward therapy. If he told her he loved her now—on his way out of town to pursue his own career—it could only distract her from all the good things that were happening for her.

A distraction like that was the last thing she needed.

During the past few days, nothing had loomed larger than his need to tell Jessica how he felt about her. But now he knew that there was something more important.

Jessica herself.

Telling her he loved her would be for his sake, not hers. It might ease the ache in his heart to let her know how he felt, but it could only create an ache in hers—whether she felt the same way or not.

So he didn't tell her. He listened to her talk about the Wildlife Foundation, and he answered her questions about his move to Chicago and the job he was taking there. A little while later, when Jessica spotted her friend Kate walking through the park and called out a hello, he used the opportunity to say his goodbyes.

"Take my seat," he told Kate when the redhead came over to the table. "I have some things I need to do." He smiled at Jessica. "We should do this again before I leave," he said.

But as he walked away, he knew that they wouldn't. Because if he saw Jessica again, he wasn't sure he'd be able to keep from spilling his guts . . . and showing her his heart.

∼

Jessica stared after Ben until he disappeared from view. Only then did she realize that Kate was talking.

She turned back toward her friend and tried to pretend she'd been listening all along. When she realized she'd missed too much, she shook her head.

"I'm sorry. I was distracted and I missed the first part of what you were saying. Would you mind repeating it?"

Her redheaded friend raised her eyebrows. "Distracted, huh? Would that have anything to do with the tall drink of water who just left? You know, the one you went on your honeymoon with?"

Jessica felt a deep blush creeping into her cheeks. "Um—"

Kate grinned at her. "It's okay, Jess. I've got eyes, and I saw the way you looked at him. But you don't have to talk about it if you don't want to."

This was the second time she'd seen Kate since getting back from Bermuda. Jessica had told her about Ben, but she'd made their trip together sound like a sexy fling.

Which was what it had been. Right?

Except that sitting and talking with Ben hadn't felt like spending time with a fling.

She opened her mouth to say something breezy—something that would let them change the subject. She could talk about the Wildlife Foundation or ask about Kate's new romance with Ian Hart or Simone's production of *A Midsummer Night's Dream* or—

"He's moving to Chicago in a few weeks," she blurted.

Kate stared at her. "Oh, Jess."

It was way too late to pretend she didn't care, but she tried anyway. "It's fine. I mean . . . we had a good time in Bermuda, and if he were staying in New York then maybe . . ."

Maybe what?

Jessica frowned down at her empty iced tea glass, replaying her conversation with Ben.

She'd been excited to tell him about the good things that were happening in her life, but not only because she wanted to share news with a friend. She'd also wanted to show Ben that whatever she felt for him wasn't because she was broken or scared or because her own life was empty, but rather—

What?

What had really been in her mind? Had she thought, deep down, that if she could show Ben she wasn't clinging to him out of fear or weakness, he'd realize they belonged together? That they should be together? That she should upend her life or he should upend his? That whatever feelings had been stirred up in Bermuda were somehow more important than everything else?

"It's not meant to be."

She spoke the words half to herself, but Kate heard them.

"You and Ben?"

She nodded. "Our lives are going in different directions. Good directions, for both of us, but different." She took a deep breath and tried to smile. "I'm sorry. Let's talk about something else."

"Like what?"

"Tell me more about you and Ian. I could use a love story with a happy ending to cheer me up."

~

Over the next few weeks she almost called Ben a hundred times. Every time she didn't, she thought he might call her.

But he didn't.

It was for the best, she told herself again and again. Talking to him would only make her want to see him, and seeing him would hurt.

But after hearing some news from Tom and Everett one day, she broke down and dialed his number.

He picked up after one ring.

"Jess," he said, and at the sound of his voice her heart squeezed in her chest.

"Hey," she said. "I haven't heard from you."

As soon as the words were out she winced. Why in the world had she said that? Now Ben would think she was being needy or something.

"I haven't heard from you, either," he said, the warmth in his voice making the words sound affectionate instead of accusatory.

It was nine o'clock at night and she was already in bed, sitting up with her back propped against the pillows. Now she slid down a little, curling up on her side with the phone pressed against her ear.

"I guess we've both been busy," she said.

"Yeah, I guess we have. How are you? How's the new job?"

"Hectic but wonderful."

"That's great. How about therapy? How's that going?"

"It's hard. I started out going three times a week, but that was too intense. I go twice a week now and it's still intense. But I'm going to stick with it." She paused, thinking about what had happened a few days ago. "I told my parents about my uncle."

"Wow. You did?"

"Yes. That was hard, too. They didn't want to believe it at first. Especially my mom, since Jeffrey was her brother. But they agreed to meet me for a session at the therapist's office, and we started to talk about it."

"I'm so proud of you, Jess."

"There's still a lot of work to do—but we've taken the first step." She rolled onto her back and switched the phone to her other ear. "So what about you? How's the packing and . . . all that?"

"Mostly done."

"Oh."

She wished she hadn't brought up packing. It was so good to hear Ben's voice that she wanted to pretend, just for a few minutes, that he wasn't moving away.

She took a deep breath. "So I actually called for a reason. Tom and Everett got married last week. They eloped, but they're going to have a reception—this Saturday at two o'clock. Would you like to be my plus one?"

There was a short silence.

"I'd love to, Jess—but that's the day I'm flying to Chicago. My plane leaves at three."

Of course it did. The universe was obviously telling her that it would be better for everyone concerned if she didn't see Ben in person again.

"Well," she said. "That's too bad. Not that you're going to Chicago," she added quickly. "Of course I'm happy about that."

"I know."

He did? What did that mean?

Probably nothing of significance. But now that she knew this was their last conversation before he moved away, everything seemed significant.

There was another silence, longer this time.

"I guess I should say good night," she said finally. "It's getting late."

"Yeah." Ben paused. "Good night, Jess."

"Good night."

CHAPTER FIFTEEN

On his last night in New York, Ben took a taxi to Jessica's neighborhood. He knew he was drifting into stalking territory, but he couldn't seem to help himself.

It wasn't like it could turn into a habit, though. He was leaving for Chicago tomorrow.

So he gave in to his desire to be near Jessica for a few hours. There was a restaurant across the street from her place, and he took an outdoor table.

Her lights were on and she was home. Every so often he saw her pass in front of the big bay window of her living room.

There was nothing stopping him from knocking on her door and seeing her in person. Nothing except the fact that if he saw her, he would tell her he loved her . . . and beg her to come to Chicago with him.

If he could be absolutely certain she would say no, he might do it. But what if she said yes?

She was starting to do work she enjoyed. Work she was passionate about. She was seeing a therapist, and she'd told her parents about the abuse she'd survived as a child.

The only thing he could accomplish by telling her how he felt was to disrupt all of that.

If she returned his feelings and agreed to come to Chicago with him, he'd be taking her away from her base of strength and the network of support she was building for herself in New York. If he offered to turn down the Chicago job and stay here in the city, she'd blame herself if things didn't work out between them.

And if she didn't return his feelings, she'd feel guilty for hurting him.

There was no good outcome here. Not for him, and not for her.

He ordered some appetizers so he could justify sitting at the table, but he wasn't hungry.

He was, however, thirsty.

He'd already had a few beers with Jamal and some other colleagues that afternoon at their favorite bar.

"You know if things don't work out in Chicago you can come back, right?" Jamal had asked. "They haven't filled your position yet. They'll be using substitutes for the first semester—and for two other openings, too. It's hard to find teachers these days."

"So you expect me to fail at the new job, huh?"

Jamal had grinned at him. "Nope. You've never failed at anything, Ben. But if you become a Bulls fan, I will fly out there and kick your ass."

"That will never happen. I'll risk life and limb by wearing my Knicks hat around town."

"That's the spirit. Barkeep, another round!"

That had been a couple of hours ago. Now he ordered a half bottle of wine to go with the appetizers he wasn't eating, because it was the kind of drink you could linger over and it wasn't hard liquor.

But it turned out that wine was just as effective at getting you drunk as scotch or vodka.

He looked up from his third glass just as Jessica passed in front of the window again.

It had been a mistake to drink. The strongest effect it was having was to shake his defenses against the need and desire that had taken hold of him.

When the bottle was empty, he decided to call it a night. He reached into his pocket for his wallet, noticing as he did so that his phone was vibrating.

It was Jessica.

He stared at the phone for a long moment. Then he turned it off, dropped bills on the table to cover his tab, and crossed the street to her apartment.

~

Ben wasn't answering his phone.

Maybe it was just as well. She didn't have a good reason for calling . . . she just wanted to hear his voice.

But she should get used to Ben not being in her life. He hadn't been for a long time, so why was it so impossible to imagine now? To come to terms with his move to Chicago?

After years of estrangement they'd had one week together, followed by six weeks of separation. How had that one week become so central to her very existence? How had it worked its way into her heart like this?

Her intercom buzzed. "Yes?"

"It's me, Jess."

An electric feeling went through her. She buzzed him in without a word and opened her door to wait for him.

The elevator doors opened and Ben was there. He stared at her like he was trying to memorize her face, and there was so much intensity and turmoil in his expression that she took a step back.

"What is it? What's wrong?"

"I can't stop thinking about you."

His voice was rough. Words and tone together sent shockwaves through her system, and her heart began to pound.

She retreated back into her apartment and he followed, closing the door behind them.

He'd been drinking; she could see that. She remembered their first night in Bermuda, when alcohol had given her the courage to kiss Ben.

What did Ben need borrowed courage to do?

Would he ask her to come with him to Chicago? If he did, what would she say?

But he didn't ask her anything. He closed the space between them and backed her against the wall, bracing his arms on either side of her.

"I'm leaving tomorrow," he said.

"I know," she said, her voice trembling.

"You can kick me out if you want to."

"Why would I want to?"

"Because I came here to sleep with you one last time, and that's a shitty thing for a man to do."

For a long moment they stared at each other, his brown eyes looking deep into her blue ones. Then she reached up and grabbed the lapels of his shirt.

"Ben?"

"Yeah?"

"Kiss me."

The kiss was different from any they'd shared in Bermuda. Hotter, darker, more desperate. She could taste wine on his tongue as he explored her mouth with carnal intensity, and it went to her head as though she'd been drinking, too.

He broke the kiss to fasten his mouth on her neck, biting and sucking as though he wanted to consume her. She let her head fall back to give him better access, moaning as waves of sensation overwhelmed her.

Suddenly he stopped. He was panting, like she was, and the ragged sound of their breathing was the only thing breaking the silence.

After a moment he pulled back, looking into her eyes again. "There's something else I want to do. Something I have no right to do."

"What?"

"I want to make love to you in your bed. I want to make it so good for you that you won't forget me. I'm a selfish bastard, Jess, and I want you to think about me after I'm gone."

She shook her head slowly, keeping her eyes on his. "Do you honestly think I won't? I've thought of you every single night since we got back from Bermuda. I've made myself come thinking about you. You've been in my bed a hundred times."

He closed his eyes and pressed his forehead against hers. "Will you let me in again?"

She grabbed his hand and pulled him down the hall toward her bedroom.

"Yes."

Once they were on her bed, they pulled each other's clothes off with frantic urgency, so hungry to be skin-to-skin they ripped fabric and tore buttons.

She almost sobbed aloud when she finally felt his naked body against hers, his chest flattening her breasts and their legs tangled together.

"I need you inside me," she gasped. "Please, Ben—"

He rolled away from her to reach down to where his pants lay in a crumpled heap. He found his wallet, pulled out a condom, and tore it open with his teeth.

In the next instant he was sheathed and crouching over her like an animal. She threw her legs open and grabbed his upper arms, marveling at the heavy bands of muscle that bunched under her hands.

"Please," she said again. "Please—"

He didn't make her wait any longer. He thrust inside her with a growl, deep and hard and perfect.

She wrapped her legs around his waist as he drove into her again and again. His pace was relentless, almost savage, and her orgasm came on her like an ocean wave in the dark. She cried out, every muscle in her body tightening, and then Ben was calling out her name as he came, too, his body pulsing inside hers.

"Wow," she said after what seemed like a long time.

Ben rolled onto his side, keeping their bodies connected as he held her close.

"Wow is right," he said. He kissed her forehead, her cheeks, her lips. "God, you're incredible."

She shook her head. "I was just trying to keep up. You're like a force of nature."

"A force of nature, huh? I like that."

She wished they could stay in each other's arms forever. But life goes on and condoms have to be thrown away, and after Ben went to the bathroom and came back the mood between them changed. He got into bed beside her and held her again, but there was a new constraint between them.

She knew what was wrong—with her, anyway. The words *I love you* were lodged in her throat, aching to be spoken, and the desire to speak warred with the need to stay silent.

Finally she couldn't take it anymore.

"You probably have to be up early tomorrow," she said.

Ben propped himself up on one elbow and looked at her. "Do you want me to leave?"

She couldn't meet his eyes. "It's not that. I mean . . . I wish you could stay." She swallowed. "But you're leaving tomorrow, and having you here . . ." Her lips trembled. "It's hard."

He nodded slowly. "Okay," was all he said. But when he leaned down and kissed her, slow and deep and sweet, he seemed to be trying to communicate something without words.

Maybe it was the same thing she couldn't say.

After he was gone and she was once again alone, she walked slowly from the living room to her bedroom doorway. She stood there for a long moment, staring at the crumpled bed sheets and wondering if they smelled like Ben. Then she went to her dresser, opened her jewelry box, and took out the dolphin necklace she'd worn every day since he'd given it to her.

She took it off every night before she went to sleep. But tonight she would sleep naked with that charm against her heart, wrapped in the sheets that smelled like the man she loved.

Chapter Sixteen

I t would be nice if you got a two-bedroom apartment," his mother said. "For when you have guests."

Ben spread cream cheese on his bagel. He was at his parents' Upper East Side apartment for a goodbye-and-good-luck breakfast before heading to the airport.

"We'll see what I can afford. How often are you planning to visit me?"

"Do I need to remind you that you're our only child?"

"Uh-huh. So, a couple times a year?"

She glared at him and he held out his hands. "I'm teasing. You guys will be welcome whenever you come."

The truth was, he was going to miss his parents a lot more than he'd ever let on.

"I still don't understand why you're going," his mother said plaintively.

"Because I want to make a difference in people's lives," he explained patiently. "This program in Chicago will reach a lot of at-risk kids, and I'd like to be a part of it."

They'd had this conversation on a regular basis ever since he'd told his parents about the new job. His mother was nothing if not persistent, and she didn't respond well to the "asked and answered" objection to a line of questioning.

"But you're already making a difference. You make a difference here. I thought you loved your job."

"I do. That's not the point."

His mother glanced at his father, who was consuming lox and capers in a detached manner with his eyes on his *Wall Street Journal*. "Feel free to jump in anytime, Seth."

"If Ben wants to go to Chicago, he can go to Chicago." He turned a page. "Horrible winters, though."

Abandoning her husband as an ally, his mother turned back to him with a sigh. "I thought Jessica might give you a reason to stay. After you went to Bermuda with her I was sure you'd come back a couple. I still can't believe nothing happened between you."

They'd had this conversation before, too, a week or so after he came back. But that time, he'd been ready for his mother's questions and his guard had been up.

This time, he wasn't ready.

He could feel his face flushing a deep red. His jaw tensed and he gripped the knife in his right hand with so much intensity that his knuckles turned white.

He couldn't meet his mother's eyes. Hoping that her eagle-eyed gaze had, for once, been looking elsewhere, he took a deep breath and forced himself to relax.

"Benjamin Taggart!"

So much for hoping.

"Look, Mom. Whatever you're thinking, just—"

She rapped her knuckles sharply on the table in front of him. "Did something happen between you and Jessica? Yes or no."

He opened his mouth to deny it. But then, unexpectedly, all the fight went out of him.

"Yeah," he said, slumping back in his chair. "It did."

Silence.

He waited for his mother to say something. To ask something. To demand further information.

But the first person who spoke was his father.

"Ben. Do you mean to say that you're involved with Jessica Bullock?"

His mother, as surprised as he was, turned her head to stare at her husband. "Seth! You don't have a problem with Jessica, do you? She's a lovely girl."

His father frowned. "I know she's a lovely girl. That's precisely my point. She's been through enough without Ben hurting her, too."

That stung. "I would never hurt Jessica. I—" He stopped.

Now his mother was staring at him. "Oh my goodness. I don't believe it."

He looked at her warily. "What?"

"You're in love with her. You're in love with Jessica Bullock."

He started to deny it, but once again the denial stuck in his throat.

He threw up his hands in defeat.

"Okay, fine. You want to hear me say it? I'm in love with Jessica. Madly, passionately, head-over-heels in love with her. But her life is here and I'm moving to Chicago, so there's no happily-ever-after to this story."

He fully expected his mother to launch into a rebuttal of biblical proportions. But once again, it was his father who spoke.

"Listen to me, Son." His father closed his paper and folded it, laying it down on the table and leaning toward him. "I stopped giving you advice a long time ago. You made it clear from the age of five that you don't want or need it. All your life you've trusted your instincts and followed your heart, and it's worked out okay."

For his father that was high praise.

"You chose the career you wanted, and I'm proud of what you've accomplished. But the one thing you've never done is make your own happiness a priority. And you know what? That's a mistake. You want to help kids, right? You want to make a difference. Well, if I've learned anything in life it's this. The best way to help other people is to be happy yourself. And if you have a chance to do that here in New York, you'd be crazy to pass it up. Jessica's a girl in a million, and you know what I think? I think you've been in love with her for years." He paused for a moment. "You'll always do the work you love, Ben. You'll find a way to help kids whether you're here or in Chicago. But if you think you'll find another woman like Jessica someplace else, you're sadly mistaken."

His father hadn't made a speech that long in years.

Ben scrubbed at his face with his hands. "You think I don't know that? But Jessica's the one I'm thinking about. She's going through a lot right now. If I change my mind about the Chicago job and stay here because of her, she'll feel responsible for that decision. That puts a hell of a lot of pressure on her."

His father spoke again. "A woman who can show up at her wedding reception after her fiancé leaves her for another man has the balls—metaphorically speaking—to handle pressure. Don't underestimate her, Ben. And don't make this decision because of what you think she can or can't deal with. That part's up to her. Make this decision the way you've always made your decisions. With your heart."

Ben dropped his hands to his sides. "But how do I know if I'm following my heart or just being selfish?"

"Now, that's always been one of your problems," his mother said.

He frowned at her. "What do you mean?"

"There's a kind of humility in being selfish once in a while. A kind of humility you could use." She folded her arms. "You've never wanted to admit you might need something you couldn't provide for yourself. You've set out to save the whole darn world—the kids you teach, and now the whole city of Chicago. You're the one who fixes other people—not the one who needs to be fixed. You help other people to be happy without thinking about yourself." She shook her head. "It takes humility to recognize that you might need someone else. That you're not the same person without them. And it takes courage to go after your own happiness."

She pushed her chair back and got to her feet. "There's something I need to get for you, Ben. No matter what you decide, it's something I want you to have."

~

He left soon afterward, noticing that time was running a little short. If he wanted to make his plane he needed to take a taxi back to his apartment, grab his bags, and get to the airport.

But instead of hailing a cab, he stood on the sidewalk in front of his parents' building and thought.

He was only two blocks from Central Park. After a moment, he turned west and started to walk.

All the arrangements had been made. His apartment was sublet, his friend would be expecting him at the Chicago airport in a few hours, and his new job would begin in a few weeks. Was he really going to blow all that up to make a play for a woman who might not want him?

Of course, he'd never hesitated to blow things up in the past if he thought it was the right thing to do. So why was he hesitating now?

There was only one explanation. One reason he was tempted to play it safe for the first time in his life.

Because he was afraid.

He wasn't sure what he was scared of. That Jessica would reject him, or that she wouldn't? That things between them wouldn't work out? That he couldn't be what she needed? That he would let her down?

Probably all of it.

But when you're faced with a fear, you have two choices: play it safe or jump off a cliff.

Ben stopped walking so abruptly that a man on a bicycle had to swerve to avoid him.

He loved Jessica. He wanted to spend the rest of his life with her.

And if he had to jump off a cliff to make that happen, then that's what he would do.

CHAPTER SEVENTEEN

Looking around Tom and Everett's reception hall, Jessica had a sudden moment of déjà vu.

Two months had gone by since the wedding day that wasn't, arguably the lowest point in her life. There had been times that day she'd worried she'd never recover. When the idea of a hopeful future—even just facing her friends and family again—had seemed impossible. The wedding she'd planned had been a stage show gone horribly wrong, an illusion exposed. A beautiful exterior with nothing inside . . . just like her.

Now here she was at another event—one that couldn't have been more different. This event meant something. And she was here, not as an empty image she was desperate to project, but as herself.

A lot of the same people were present: friends, family, acquaintances. But her relationships with those people were more honest now, even if they were more difficult.

When her parents had shown up today, the sight of them had brought tears to her eyes.

Two months ago she'd felt empty, weak, humiliated, shattered. Now she felt strong and purposeful. Hopeful. Alive.

Or at least, she did until Tom came over to the table she was sharing with Vicki and Kate. Jessica had hoped that Simone would be there, too, but she was in Ireland—having what sounded like an incredible adventure with a sexy British director.

Tom kissed her on the cheek. "I would've asked you to be my best man if we'd had a formal wedding. Instead, I hope you'll give a toast later on. Will you?"

A twinge of anxiety tightened her belly. "I don't know, Tom. You know I don't like speaking in public. I'm afraid I'll just embarrass you."

"You can't be serious."

"What do you mean?"

"Unless you actually burn the place down, I can promise you won't embarrass me as much as I embarrassed you at our wedding. You do remember that, don't you?"

She found herself grinning. "I have a vague recollection."

"Okay, then. What do you say? It would really mean a lot to Everett and me," he added more seriously.

How could she say no?

"All right," she said. "I'll give a short toast."

He kissed her on the cheek again. "Thanks, Jessica."

Two months ago, it felt like her life had ended. Now here she was joking with Tom about that disastrous wedding day and celebrating the true love in his life.

Celebrating who he really was.

But though she was genuinely happy for Tom, there was an ache behind her breastbone that hadn't gone away since Ben left last night. In spite of the joyful celebration all around her, the fact that she was surrounded by friends and family that she could, finally, meet on honest terms, there was something missing.

The man she loved.

But she had to let him go. Didn't she? His future was in Chicago, and she wanted good things for him as fiercely as he wanted them for her.

She wouldn't ask him to change who he was, or to abandon the life he'd chosen. Because he would never, ever ask that of her.

She was tempted to partake of liquid courage before the toasts began, but she found to her surprise that she didn't really need it. When it was her turn to speak, she hadn't yet touched her champagne.

"I've known Tom for half my life, and he's one of the most wonderful people I've ever met. I don't know Everett nearly as well, but he gave me a job when I needed one, so I'm sort of obligated to say I like him, too." A ripple of laughter from the audience. "Some of you were here the last time the three of us participated in a wedding. I'm here to tell you that after this one, your gifts won't be returned." Another laugh.

Okay, this wasn't so bad. She was starting to feel almost confident.

She opened her mouth to continue, but there was an interruption. The door to the function room opened and Ben Taggart walked in.

For a moment she couldn't believe her eyes. He was supposed to be on a plane to Chicago. Like, right now.

Goose bumps swept over her skin. They stared at each other across the room as though no one else were there, and in that moment Jessica had an epiphany.

She took a deep breath and let it out. Then she lifted her chin and went on with her toast.

"Tom and I have a lot in common—both good things and bad. We haven't always been brave, and we haven't always been honest. But both of us have been blessed with people in our lives who *are* brave and honest. People who believe in us more than we believe in ourselves."

She looked down at Tom and Everett. "These two found each other in a world that hasn't made it easy. I admire them both more than I can say." She held up her champagne flute. "Please raise your glasses to the adorable couple."

"To the adorable couple!" the crowd called out, and everybody drank.

Then Jessica cleared her throat. "That pretty much takes care of my toast. But with Tom and Everett's permission, there's something else I'd like to say."

Not everyone had noticed Ben standing at the back of the room, but Tom had. He looked from her to Ben and back again, and a smile spread across his face.

"Go for it, Jess."

Warmth flooded through her. Standing up in front of all these people—friends, family, acquaintances, strangers—she had another moment of déjà vu.

Two months ago she'd faced a crowd like this. But this time, she didn't feel trapped and powerless and afraid of herself.

She felt strong and free and clear-sighted. And for the first time in her life, she knew exactly what she wanted to say.

"Maybe Tom and I would have figured things out on our own—eventually. But luckily for us, we didn't have to. Tom had Everett, who loved him so much he crashed a wedding to stop him from making a terrible mistake. And I have someone, too. A man named Ben Taggart."

At that point, the people in the room who hadn't noticed the new arrival swiveled their heads to see who she was looking at.

Ben didn't seem to be aware of them. He was staring at her like she was the only person in the room.

The only person in the world.

"I love you," she said. "You might not have a savior complex, but you did save me. You helped me know myself and believe in myself. That's always been your gift. It's what makes you such an amazing teacher—and such an amazing man." She took a breath. "I've never felt like I have much to give. My love, my courage, my strength . . . it all feels like a work in progress. But even though my heart seems small when I compare it to yours, it's the only one I have. And it's yours, Ben. It's yours forever."

There was a moment of silence. Then, as Ben crossed the space between them, everyone in the room began to clap and cheer.

The cheering grew louder when he took her in his arms and kissed her. Under the cover of the applause he murmured in her ear, "Do you think they'll mind if I take you away for a little while? As long as I promise to bring you back?"

"Who cares what anyone else thinks?" she asked blithely. "Let's go." She smiled at Tom. "We'll be back," she said.

Tom waved his hand. "Take your time."

She grabbed Ben by the hand and led him out of the room. There was a velvet-covered bench in the hallway and she pulled him down onto it.

He slid his hands into her hair, gazing into her eyes.

She basked in the joy of being with him. "I thought you were on your way to Chicago."

"I changed my mind." He took a deep breath. "You're my soul mate. I want to spend the rest of my life with you, Jess—right here in New York City." He grinned at her. "And after your speech, I know you feel the same way. You said you love me in front of a roomful of people. You made a spectacle of yourself."

"I know. But it's just one of the many things I've done lately that I never thought I'd do."

Ben started to say something, and then he blinked. "Damn! I almost forgot."

"Forgot what?"

He reached into his pocket. "I never thought I'd do anything both of my parents wanted me to do. But it turns out I was wrong, because they think I should do this. And they gave me something to help the cause. It belonged to my great-grandmother on my mother's side."

He pulled a ring box from his pocket and opened it. A vintage Edwardian-cut diamond winked at her, brilliant against a black velvet background.

Jessica stared at it for a long moment.

"If you're going all traditional on me, you should get down on one knee," she said, trying to sound sassy and failing miserably.

"I'm only doing this because I worship you," he said, sliding off the bench and kneeling at her feet. "Not because I'm traditional."

Her eyes filled with tears. "You can't worship me. *I* worship *you.*"

He took her hands in his and kissed them. "Say yes, Jessica. Say yes and let me put this ring on your finger. Then we can plan a wedding . . . and a honeymoon."

She pulled her hands from his, but only so she could wipe the tears from her cheeks. "Another one, huh?"

He smiled up at her, his face so dear and so beloved that she never wanted to look at anything else. "Is that a yes?" he asked.

She started to answer and hiccupped.

"I didn't quite catch that," Ben said gravely.

Now she was laughing and crying at the same time. "Yes, darn you. Yes, yes, yes!"

" 'Yes, darn you.' Is that really what you want to go with? The story we tell our grandkids?"

"They'll think it's adorable. Are you going to put that on me, or what?"

He slid the ring onto her finger. "So about that honeymoon. Do you have any ideas?"

Her tears were still falling, and she couldn't stop smiling. "Yes, actually. What about you?"

"I think anyplace we go together will be paradise. But I do have one particular spot in mind."

"Bermuda?"

"Bermuda."

"I love you, Ben."

"I love you, too."

EPILOGUE

D o you remember when the three of us met for the first time?"
Jessica asked.

She and Kate and Simone were on beach chairs waiting for
Zach and Ben to return with their rum swizzles. Ian and his nephew
Jacob were snorkeling in the ocean.

Simone nodded. "Freshman year of college, move-in day." She
grinned suddenly. "If you'd told me then that we'd end up friends—and
that we'd still be friends ten years later—I would've said you were nuts."

"I honestly don't know why the two of you stayed friends with
me," Jessica said, tilting her face toward the sun. "I was a bitch
ninety percent of the time."

Kate smiled at her. "You weren't that bad. Seventy percent tops."
Her eyes grew misty. "Do you remember when my grandmother
passed away the summer after junior year? I was devastated. You
were in Monte Carlo with your family, but you dropped everything
and flew back to be with me."

Jessica felt embarrassed. "You would have done the same for
me. In a heartbeat." She looked out at the ocean to where Ian and
Jacob were floating. "How is the TV show coming?" Kate and Jacob
had collaborated on a project last year, and it was scheduled to pre-
miere in a few months.

"It's going great," Kate said, smiling to herself. "Jacob is so
excited."

Simone smacked her on the arm. "What's up with the smirk? What aren't you telling us?"

"Nothing. Well . . . nothing official. I just think there's a chance that Ian might—"

Jessica squealed. "He's going to propose!"

"I don't know for sure. But Jacob is terrible at keeping secrets, and he's been making veiled hints since we got here. You guys did say you'd keep him company tonight, right? Ian made a dinner reservation for the two of us."

"Yeah, he's definitely going to propose." Simone looked around at the gorgeous vista. "He couldn't have picked a more romantic spot. It's given me a million ideas for the new production Zach and I are planning. Did you know *The Tempest* was inspired by a British shipwreck right here in Bermuda?" She leaned back in her chair. "It's no wonder you and Ben fell in love here, Jess. If I weren't already in love with Zach, this place would have done the trick."

Kate agreed. "It is pretty spectacular. I'm so glad you invited us here to celebrate with you—although I'm still a little disappointed that you guys eloped."

"Are you kidding?" Simone asked. "After the way her last wedding went, Jessica was entitled to do whatever she wanted this time around. And eloping is romantic." She shook her head. "I can't believe you were the first one of us to get married, though. I was sure it would be Kate."

Zach and Ben came walking across the sand. As always, the sight of her husband made Jessica's heart beat a little faster.

"I've known Ben most of my life," she said. "Once I finally figured out that I loved him, there was nothing else to wait for."

Ben set down their drinks and leaned over to kiss her.

"Happy?" he asked.

Tears came into her eyes as she kissed him back.

"So happy."

ACKNOWLEDGMENTS

Thanks to the amazing team at Montlake, especially Maria Gomez. Thanks also to Nicci Jordan Hubert for her hard work and insight. And as always, my deepest gratitude to Mikel Strom, Tara Gorvine, and Melissa Chalmers for their help and encouragement, and to my son Owen for his patience. You guys are the best.

ABOUT THE AUTHOR

Abigail Strom started writing stories at the age of seven and has never been able to stop. On her way to becoming a full-time writer, she earned a BA in English from Cornell University as well as an MFA in dance from the University of Hawaii. Abigail has held a wide variety of jobs from dance teacher and choreographer to human resource manager. Now she works in her pajamas and lives in New England with her family, who are incredibly supportive of the hours she spends hunched over her computer.